"It's so exciting!" Jessica gushed. "I can't believe someone in our class is getting *married*."

"Jess," Elizabeth said sharply. "I don't think you realize how serious this whole thing is. Maria's only sixteen, and Michael can't be much older!"

"Who cares?" Jessica asked.

Elizabeth sighed. She wished she could be as enthusiastic about Maria and Michael's engagement as everyone else at Sweet Valley High.

"Hey," Jessica said, "maybe cheerleading practice won't be so bad after all. We'll be able to pump Maria and find out everything about the wedding—when Michael popped the question, whether he got her a ring, and all the important stuff."

"Right," Elizabeth said ironically. "No point in worrying about trivial things like what they're going to do about the fact that their parents don't even know they're dating."

"You don't have a romantic bone in your body!" Jessica accused.

"I just don't see what's romantic about a secret engagement, that's all," Elizabeth replied. She didn't know Maria or Michael very well, but she hoped more than anything that they knew what they were doing!

Bantam Books in the Sweet Valley High series
Ask your bookseller for the books you have missed

SWEET VALLEY HIGH

FORBIDDEN LOVE

Written by
Kate William

Created by
FRANCINE PASCAL

BANTAM BOOKS
NEW YORK · TORONTO · LONDON · SYDNEY · AUCKLAND

RL 6, IL age 12 and up

FORBIDDEN LOVE

A Bantam Book / February 1987

Sweet Valley High is a trademark of Francine Pascal
Conceived by Francine Pascal
Produced by Daniel Weiss Associates, Inc.
33 West 17th Street
New York, NY 10011
Cover art by James Mathewuse

ISBN 0-553-27521-6

Published simultaneously in the United States and Canada.

Bantam Books are published by Bantam Books, a division of Bantam Doubleday Dell Publishing Group, Inc. Its trademark, consisting of the words "Bantam Books" and the portrayal of a rooster, is Registered in U.S. Patent and Trademark Office and in other countries. Marca Registrada. Bantam Books, 666 Fifth Avenue, New York, New York 10103.

PRINTED IN THE UNITED STATES OF AMERICA

OPM   16   15   14   13   12   11   10   9   8   7

FORBIDDEN LOVE

One

"I can't believe it," Jessica Wakefield grumbled. She tossed her silky, sun-streaked blond hair off her shoulder. "A gorgeous Friday afternoon, and Ricky Capaldo has to call a special cheerleading practice!"

Elizabeth stretched luxuriously, ignoring the plaintive note in her twin sister's voice. The last period of the school day had just ended, and she and her sister were relaxing on the emerald green lawn in front of Sweet Valley High. Elizabeth was waiting for her best friend, Enid Rollins, to emerge from the school, and Jessica was waiting for cheerleading practice to begin. Jessica didn't usually mind practice. Cheerleading was one of her favorite activities, especially since the squad had purchased new uniforms with short, pleated skirts. Jessica knew she looked terrific in her uniform, and she loved cheering

1

in front of big crowds. But she felt Friday afternoon was a better time to relax on the beach than work on routines on the football field. She scrunched her face up in exasperation, and Elizabeth burst out laughing.

"What's wrong with you, Jess?" she asked. "You look like you're trying to turn yourself inside out!"

Jessica eyed her twin loftily. "I happen to be thinking, Liz," she retorted. "Can't you tell?"

Elizabeth suppressed an urge to laugh. Sometimes she couldn't believe she and Jessica were twins. True, with their blue-green eyes, sun-streaked hair, and big smiles, they were mirror images of each other. Their willowy, five-foot-six-inch frames were similar enough to allow them to trade clothing, even though Elizabeth dressed much more conservatively than Jessica. But choice of clothes was only one way in which they were opposites. Take cheerleading, for instance. The last thing Elizabeth would ever do voluntarily would be to jump around in front of a bunch of strangers. Elizabeth wasn't shy, but she liked her privacy. She preferred activities where she could use her mind. Her favorite hobby was writing, and she devoted hours every week to *The Oracle*, Sweet Valley High's newspaper. "Slow and steady" was one of Elizabeth's favorite mottoes. She disliked change.

Unlike Jessica, she could not see the appeal of changing fashions every ten seconds, racing from one boyfriend to the next, or throwing herself into new hobbies with dizzying speed. Elizabeth liked to have fun as much as her twin, but her energies were more likely to be devoted to fund-raising projects, community activities, or relaxing with a few close friends.

Here, too, the twins differed. Jessica's friends were mostly girls she knew from cheerleading or Pi Beta Alpha, the exclusive sorority both she and Elizabeth belonged to. Elizabeth thought most of the sorority girls were snobs. She much preferred Enid's quiet companionship and the solid, affectionate relationship she had with her boyfriend, Jeffrey French. Elizabeth didn't mind leaving the dazzle and theatrics to her twin.

"Hey," Jessica said, her eyes brightening as she focused on a small, dark girl coming out of the main doors of school. "There's Maria!"

Elizabeth followed her gaze. Brown-haired, pretty Maria Santelli was a junior, like the twins. Recently she had been the subject of a great deal of gossip. "Have you found out yet whether or not it's true?" she asked. "Are Maria and Michael really engaged?"

Jessica hugged her knees with excitement. "It's so wonderful!" she gushed. "I can't believe someone in our very own class is getting

3

married." Her expression was dreamy. "I wonder if I'll get to be a bridesmaid. I can wear flowers in my hair and everything—and maybe I'll catch the bouquet!"

"Jess," Elizabeth said sharply, "I don't think you realize how serious this whole thing is. There's more to marriage than just a ring and a wedding. Maria's only sixteen, and Michael can't be much more than seventeen!" Michael Harris was a senior. He and Maria had been dating, but no one could have imagined they would be getting engaged!

"Who cares?" Jessica responded. "Mr. Collins says Juliet was only fourteen when she met Romeo. Age," she added authoritatively, "has nothing to do with anything."

Elizabeth sighed. She wished she could be as enthusiastic about Maria and Michael's engagement as everyone else seemed to be. Not that either Maria or Michael had yet confirmed the rumor that was spreading around school like wildfire. Elizabeth couldn't help hoping that it was only that, a rumor. Cara Walker, one of Jessica's best friends and the girlfriend of the twins' brother Steven, had broken the news to the twins a few days before. Characteristically Jessica had been instantly excited. Maria was a cheerleader, but Jessica had never been very

4

close to her. Now she acted as though Maria were her best friend.

"Hey," Jessica said, leaning forward and craning her neck to follow Maria's progress across the lawn and down the footpath to the athletic field, "maybe practice won't be bad after all. We'll be able to pump Maria and find out everything about it—when Michael popped the question, whether he got her a ring, and all the important stuff."

Elizabeth shook her head. "Right," she said sarcastically. "No point in worrying about trivial things like what they're going to do about the fact that their parents don't even know they're dating!"

The Santellis and the Harrises had been bitter enemies since a business venture had soured years before. They had forbidden their children to see each other.

Jessica looked sober. "Isn't it exciting," she said, her eyes widening as she considered Michael and Maria's predicament. "Liz, don't you wish Jeffrey's parents were feuding with Mom and Dad? Don't you think it would make everything more *interesting* between you two?"

Elizabeth spotted Enid coming out of school and waved at her friend. "No," she told her twin firmly. "I don't think Jeffrey and I need a feud to make things interesting, but thanks for the suggestion!"

Jessica looked hurt. "I don't get it," she said. "My own flesh and blood, and you don't have a romantic bone in your body!"

"I just don't see what's romantic about a secret engagement, that's all," Elizabeth replied, getting to her feet. She didn't know Maria very well, but everything she had heard about her relationship with Michael worried Elizabeth. She hoped they knew what they were doing.

"Well, I'm going to practice. I'm going to find out the whole story," Jessica declared. She jumped to her feet and grabbed the hot-pink nylon duffel filled with her gear. "See you later."

Elizabeth sighed as her sister raced off. She could always count on one thing: Wherever the excitement was, Jessica was bound to be right in the thick of it. And Maria and Michael's engagement was the hottest thing to hit Sweet Valley High in months!

Enid and Elizabeth were strolling home together, enjoying the balmy, cloudless Southern California afternoon and discussing the events of the week. Enid Rollins was an attractive brown-haired girl with an open, friendly expression. She and Elizabeth had been best friends for quite a while and were often able to guess what was on each other's minds. "What do you think of the new social studies project?" Enid asked, her green eyes twinkling. "It seems like everyone has marriage on the brain these days!"

Elizabeth chuckled. As part of a social studies unit, some juniors and seniors were going to take part in a special seminar on family and marriage. Mr. Jaworski, a history teacher who would lead the discussions, had proposed the seminar to introduce students to some of the issues adults face in day-to-day life. Students would be paired up into "husband and wife" teams on Monday. Each couple would be given a folder containing information about their social status, income, and occupation. They would be given a set of facts about their imaginary family: how many children they had, what ages they were, their names, whether they had any special problems. The family and marriage unit would last two weeks, though they would spend time on it only every other day. Each pair would be given test problems to work out, and at the end of each hour, one couple would be chosen to report how they had worked through the problem, what additional problems they had encountered, and what they had learned from the experiment.

"I think it's a good idea," Elizabeth said enthusiastically. "I was trying to tell Jessica that, but she wouldn't listen," she added. "It seems like a good thing to talk about some of the aspects of marriage people don't really consider. The day to day, nitty-gritty stuff."

"Jeffrey's in our seminar," Enid teased her friend. "Maybe you two will get teamed up."

"So are Maria and Michael," Elizabeth said, frowning. "What do you think of this whole business about their engagement?"

"Well, I don't know that much about it," Enid said. "But I thought that Maria was forbidden even to go out with Michael. I thought their parents were bitter enemies or something."

"I thought so, too. In fact I'm pretty sure that's true," Elizabeth said. "It seems a little rash to get engaged, don't you think?"

Enid pushed her brown hair away from her face, a sign she was deep in thought. "Part of me thinks it's pretty romantic," she admitted. "But I can see a million problems. They're awfully young, for one thing."

"It's funny," Elizabeth mused. "Maria seems to have so many plans. She brought some material to the *Oracle* office the other day for an Outward Bound project she wants to organize this summer. She said she needed to get a certain number of kids for it to get off the ground. Do you think she'll be able to do that if she and Michael get married?"

"I don't know," Enid answered. "She does seem like someone who has a lot of commitments. She's got cheerleading and the sorority, and she's been helping Winston run for Student Council PTA representative."

Elizabeth looked interested. "I didn't know he was running," she commented. Winston Egbert, a tall, lanky junior with dark hair, was the acknowledged class clown. He hardly seemed to be the type who would be interested in serving as liaison between the Student Council and the Parent-Teacher Association. A few students had already put themselves in the running for the spot, which Elizabeth knew was an important one. And now that she'd thought about it, she realized that Winston wasn't a bad choice at all. He was hardworking and earnest and would give his all to whatever he chose to do.

"I heard Maria telling Olivia Davidson about it yesterday," Enid said. "Apparently it's something he really wants. Only he doesn't have much confidence, not when it comes to something as serious as this. So Maria's been helping him out. She's on the council and has been giving him pointers. She's his official manager. She's making posters for him, helping him with his campaign speech, things like that."

Elizabeth didn't say anything for a minute. It seemed to her that by getting engaged to Michael Harris, Maria Santelli was making an enormous mistake. She seemed to be such an energetic, ambitious girl. She had her whole life in front of her. Why get married in her junior year of high school?

And what about Michael? Elizabeth didn't know him at all. He was on the tennis team, a tall, athletic guy with dark hair and warm hazel eyes. He had a healthy suntan, was well groomed, and had a slightly studious air that had always appealed to Elizabeth. He seemed like a perfectly nice guy. A nice guy—but a *husband*?

It almost seemed too crazy to believe! But it wasn't her business, Elizabeth reminded herself. She was sure Maria and Michael knew what they were doing. After all, they had known each other for years.

Still, she couldn't help feeling curious. And she couldn't help looking forward to the report she knew her twin would have when she returned from cheerleading practice.

"Do you have any idea how gorgeous you are?" Jeffrey French said in a husky voice. He leaned over and traced one of Elizabeth's eyebrows with his finger. The afternoon sun was beginning to fade, and the two were swinging together in the new hammock Mr. Wakefield had hung between two trees in the Wakefields' backyard. Prince Albert, the Wakefields' new golden retriever puppy, was sound asleep on Elizabeth's lap.

"Who?" Elizabeth said teasingly. "Prince Albert or me?" But her eyes misted over a little despite the light tone of her voice. She loved it when Jeffrey had that little catch in his voice.

"You're pretty special yourself," she murmured, resting her head on his chest. She had always thought Jeffrey was incredibly good-looking; but that afternoon he looked more handsome than usual. He had a deep tan, and his green eyes glowed. His thick blond hair was bleaching out a little, too. And he looked so strong—and so protective! Elizabeth sighed with contentment. Overhead the leaves glinted with fading sunlight. "I feel so safe," Elizabeth murmured, stroking Prince Albert's head with her hand. "Jeffrey," she added softly, "do you ever think about getting married?"

Jeffrey was quiet for a minute. "Sure," he said at last. "I think about it sometimes. I try to picture where I'm going to live and what my kids will look like. . . ."

Elizabeth felt funny. She and Jeffrey had been a couple for a while now, but they'd never had a conversation like this before. She felt strangely nervous bringing it up, but the matter-of-fact tone in Jeffrey's voice reassured her. "But you think about it as something way down the road, don't you?" she asked.

Jeffrey chuckled. "You're not proposing to me, are you?" he teased.

Elizabeth slapped his arm lightly. "Fat chance," she joked. "No. I was just thinking about Maria and Michael, that's all."

"Mmm," Jeffrey murmured. "Strange, isn't it? I wonder what the story is."

Elizabeth stared up at the leaves overhead, quiet contentment washing over her. She wondered too. But now she felt so peaceful she didn't care about anything but being right where she was. She was about to tell Jeffrey how she felt, but he silenced her by leaning over and covering her lips with his. The next minute Prince Albert woke up with a squeal as Jeffrey leaned on him. Elizabeth started laughing.

"Darned dog," Jeffrey complained. But he was too busy smiling at Elizabeth to think about Prince Albert for long.

Two

"Come on, girls!" Ricky Capaldo cried. "We've got to get the pyramid right this afternoon. Everyone line up, and let's figure out who's going to go where."

Ricky was the cheerleaders' manager. A short, energtic boy with an endless fund of humor, he had worked hard to make the squad as good as it was. There were eight cheerleaders in all. Jessica and Robin Wilson were co-captains. Jessica's friend Cara Walker was also on the team, along with Maria, Jeanie West, Sandra Bacon, Ricky's ex-girlfriend Annie Whitman, and the newest member of the team, Amy Sutton. Amy had been Elizabeth's best friend in sixth grade, but they had lost touch after Amy's family moved to the East Coast. When the Suttons came back to Sweet Valley, Elizabeth and Amy found they had grown in different directions. Elizabeth found Amy boy-crazy and irresponsible, whereas Jessica thought she was tons of fun. Jessica had been instrumental in getting Amy on the team. Now Amy, Cara, and Jessica were inseparable at practice. That afternoon they came out of the locker room together, buzzing with excitement about Maria.

"Who's going to ask her about it?" Amy asked, pulling her blond hair back in a ponytail. "Cara, I think you should. You're the one she confided in."

"No way," Cara objected. "Maria made me promise to keep it secret. I can't ask her about it in front of all of you."

"I know!" Jessica exclaimed. "I'll just happen to grab her hand when we're getting into the pyramid formation, and I'll ask her about the ring."

"Come on," Cara urged her. "Ricky's waving at us. I think we're late."

As it turned out, Jessica and Amy had nothing to worry about. Maria was surrounded by the rest of the squad, her left hand extended. A small, perfectly round diamond twinkled on her third finger. The band was slender and gold, very simple. It was beautiful.

"Maria, it's gorgeous!" Robin Wilson exclaimed, leaning over Maria's hand to admire the ring. "I can't believe he really gave you a diamond."

"Well, we *are* engaged," Maria said.

Jessica and Amy crowded in to see the ring. "You mean it's all out in the open now?" Amy asked, staring at Maria's hand.

Maria's face reddened. "Well—not really. I mean, we're telling our friends. But we're not letting our parents know—not for now, anyway. So keep it quiet," she added meaningfully.

Jessica stared at the ring, watching the sunlight shoot through the gem, making fiery sparkles of light. "What a beautiful ring," she said. "Maria, tell us how it happened. When did he ask you?"

Maria tossed back her hair, clearly enjoying the attention. She was a pretty girl, but that afternoon she seemed truly beautiful; there was something different about her, a new spirit, a new kind of excitement. Her eyes glowed, and her cheeks were flushed with excitement. "I'll tell you," she said dramatically, "but remember, not a word of it to your parents." Her large eyes narrowed momentarily. "My parents would absolutely kill me if they found out."

"Before you tell us how you two got engaged, would you just explain what the deal is between your parents and the Harrises?" Robin Wilson asked.

Maria sighed. "It's a real mess. It's kind of a long story," she added, looking nervously at Ricky.

"Go on," Ricky said, obviously too interested to remind them about practicing.

"Well, Michael's father and my father used to be partners," Maria began. "They went to college together and were really close. They formed the business partnership ten years ago. They did everything together. They played tennis, socialized together, worked together—they even joked about Michael and me. They thought it would be great if we grew up and fell in love." Maria's expression grew serious. "Anyway, four years ago they had a huge fight. I can't really go into it now. It's all too complicated. The important thing is that their friendship—and their business partnership—ended then and there. It was awful for all of us. The next thing we knew was they stopped speaking. It all had to do with a big deal they were trying to put together. The deal fell through, they split up their partnership, and I was told we weren't ever going to see the Harrises again." She was quiet for a minute. "Well, a few months ago Michael and I ended up working on a project for the film society together. We hadn't spoken in years. We were really weird around each other at first, and then we found out we still liked each other. A lot. Only by then we weren't kids anymore." She blushed happily. "And the rest is history. We've been going out ever since."

"But what about your parents?" Jessica demanded. "How do they feel about the whole thing?"

Maria set her jaw stubbornly. "They found out about it and told us to stop seeing each other. I thought we should bring it out in the open, but Michael didn't want to upset his dad. So we just continued to meet anyway, without them knowing." She smiled sadly. "They think we broke up."

"Where do you tell them you go when you and Michael go out?" Amy asked, fascinated.

"They think I have a boyfriend named Josh," Maria told her. "I hate lying," she added, "but they're being so unreasonable. What else can we do?"

"When do you plan to let them know?" Robin asked. "Haven't your parents asked you about your ring?"

Maria looked embarrassed. "I take it off when I get home and keep it in my pocket," she admitted. "Just for now. We're planning to tell them all soon," she added. "We just need a little more time to get them prepared."

"So tell us how it happened," Amy cajoled. "We want to know all about it, every last detail."

Maria's face filled with joy. Clearly this was the part of the story she preferred to dwell on. "You wouldn't believe it," she murmured, looking with admiration at her ring as it twinkled in the sunlight. "You have no idea how wonderful it is to be engaged. When Michael asked me . . ."

"Where were you?" Jessica asked. "Did he take you somewhere really romantic?"

"We were at Secca Lake," Maria reminisced dreamily. "We were parked there, watching the stars and everything. It was a really gorgeous night, and there was all this moonlight on the water. The whole lake looked silvery. You know what I mean?"

The group of girls around her was entranced, listening to her every word with fascination. Even Ricky seemed unable to interrupt.

"Anyway, it was perfectly quiet. There was nothing moving, just the lake in front of us, all silvery and calm. Michael kept staring at me, and I felt really self-conscious." Maria played with the ring, her eyes wide as she recollected the scene. "We had been talking really seriously for a long time about all sorts of things, including the future. Then all of a sudden he took a box out of the glove compartment and opened it and handed it to me." She closed her eyes briefly, and when she opened them again, they were shining with tears of happiness. "I couldn't believe it!"

"But what did he say?" Amy prompted her. "Did he ask you, or just put the ring on your finger?"

"He asked me," Maria said. "He said some things I can't repeat, and then he kissed me, and then he asked me if I'd wear the ring—if I'd marry him."

Robin Wilson gasped, and the tension was broken as everyone giggled. "It's so exciting," Robin said apologetically. "I'm sorry, Maria. Go on."

Jessica pretended to swoon. "That," she said dramatically, "is the most romantic thing I've ever heard in my entire *life*!"

"Me, too!" Annie Whitman exclaimed. She blushed a little as she caught Ricky's eye. She and Ricky used to date, and though they were still good friends, Annie found it embarrassing sometimes to talk about romance in front of him.

"It *is* romantic," agreed Ricky. "But I think, as your manager, that you girls really need to stop thinking about romance and rings and start thinking about your pyramid formation. There's a big soccer game coming up, and you don't want to look terrible, do you?"

"I want to be next to Maria," Jessica declared.

"Me, too!" everyone else exclaimed, pushing closer to the tiny brunette.

Maria's eyes were shining as brightly as the diamond on her left hand. She loved telling them about Michael. As far as she was concerned, becoming engaged was the best thing that had ever happened to her!

"Boy, Ricky sure knows how to tire a girl out," Annie grumbled as she and Maria crossed the parking lot.

Maria nodded agreement, barely hearing her friend's complaint. She was scanning the parking lot for Michael's Trans-Am. "There he is!" she said aloud, her face lighting up. "Annie, I've got to run," she added apologetically, tossing her duffel bag over one shoulder and hurrying off without looking back.

"Hey," she said happily, throwing her bag in the car and climbing in after it. She kissed Michael on the cheek and patted his arm. "Do you have any idea how good it is to see you?" she asked, her voice husky.

"Probably about as good as it is to see *you*," Michael told her.

Maria felt a surge of pride as she regarded Michael. She loved the way he looked. He was well-built, though slender. His dark hair was neat and short. She liked his glasses, too, especially the way they slid down his nose when he played tennis. And he had the sweetest sprinkling of freckles on his nose. "I still can't believe it," she murmured as he started the motor.

"Believe what?" he asked, grinning.

"Believe we're engaged, you dope." She giggled. "I told the squad. You should have seen their faces!"

Michael's eyes darkened. "Hey, I thought this was supposed to be a secret," he objected. "No offense to some of your squad members, but they're not exactly famous for their discretion. Between Jessica and Cara and Amy Sutton—"

"They promised not to tell," Maria protested, feeling hurt. "I made them." She toyed with the door handle for a minute. "Anyway, what's the point of being engaged if we can't tell anyone about it?"

Michael sighed. "We've been through all of this before. We'll tell people eventually. Just not now!"

Maria bit her lip for a moment. "Oh, never mind!" she exclaimed. "I don't want to argue with you. I'd hate to end up like Kate and Richard."

Kate was Michael's older sister. She was twenty-three and was supposed to marry Richard that summer. But all they ever seemed to do was argue. Maria hadn't seen Richard and

Kate together in ages, ever since the Harrises and the Santellis had their falling out. But she could remember their arguments from the old days. And she heard enough about their fighting now from Michael to be sure that theirs was a relationship she couldn't bear to be in.

"You're not fair about Kate," Michael objected. "She and Richard just have their own way of dealing with things."

"Well, just the same, I'd hate to deal with things the way they do." Maria shuddered, as she remembered the terrible fights Kate and Richard had had. "We won't be like that, will we?"

"Of course not!" Michael said, leaning over and patting her leg.

Maria was thoughtful as he drove her home. She felt strange about having made a critical comment about anyone in Michael's family. By some unspoken agreement, Michael always made a point of defending her parents, and she defended his. Whenever they talked about their parents, each took the other's side. She had never made a negative comment about anyone in his family before that remark about Kate. It wasn't a big deal, but it struck her as strange.

"What do you want to do this weekend?" Michael asked her. "You feel like seeing a movie tonight?"

Maria thought about it for a moment, then said, "Whatever you want to do." They were nearing Orange Street, and she knew any minute he would slow down, park, and let her out. They always stopped here, and she walked the last two blocks. Her parents both worked, but her little sister, Diane, got home early and if she saw Michael's Trans-Am . . .

Maria felt a lump form in her throat. She hated sneaking around this way. Sometimes she felt she couldn't stand it a minute longer. It seemed so unfair! Why couldn't she and Michael just go out the way other people did?

"Hey," Michael was saying softly, "are you OK?"

Suddenly the lump melted. "I'm fine," Maria murmured, lifting her face for his kiss. She forgot all about sneaking around then. It was enough to feel him near her, enough to realize that they belonged to each other now and forever and ever.

"Should I pick you up right here at eight?" he asked.

Maria nodded, reluctantly turning away from him. *But he's mine, really mine. We're engaged,* she reminded herself as she opened the car door and slid out. Michael was her fiancé. Before she closed the car door, she stuck her head inside and said softly, "I love you, Michael."

Michael leaned over and kissed her lightly. "I love you, too, Maria. See you tonight."

Maria nodded, then closed the car door.

"Fiancé," she said aloud as she walked slowly down the street. Michael beeped the car's horn once, waved, and pulled away from the curb. Maria watched him go in silence. Everything was happening so fast!

She couldn't remember ever being so happy. She just wished she didn't have to lie to her parents. Slowly she headed toward her house, trying to decide where to tell them Josh was taking her that night.

Three

"Today," Mr. Jaworski announced, his eyes twinkling behind his tortoiseshell glasses, "is the first day of our family and marriage seminar." The group broke into giggles as they watched him riffle through the tiny scraps of paper in the box on his desk. "Now, you all understand the rules. There are twenty-four of you, twelve boys and twelve girls. Each boy's name is written on a slip of paper in this box. And each girl will now come up to the front of the room and draw"—he cleared his throat dramatically—"the man who will be your husband for the next two weeks—in the seminar, that is."

Everyone laughed, and the girls got up and formed a line. Jessica drew first, and the class burst into applause when she read the slip of paper aloud: "Winston Egbert."

Elizabeth drew Bruce Patman, who gave her

a big wink as she pronounced his name. She couldn't help smiling at the prospect of pretending to be married to one of the richest boys in the school. In the old days Bruce would have been a pain to work with, she thought. He used to have an ego problem. But his relationship with Regina Morrow had mellowed him, and she thought their "marriage" would be fun.

The rest of the girls drew their names fairly quickly. Olivia Davidson drew Jeffrey. She smiled at Elizabeth. "I promise not to get carried away," she whispered to Elizabeth when she returned to her seat. Lila Fowler, the spoiled daughter of a computer magnate, looked less than thrilled when she was assigned to Bill Chase, whom she secretly found a little dull. But no one paid any attention to Lila. The group was too busy watching Maria's face as she reached for her slip, the third to last in the box. Michael's name hadn't been chosen yet. Word had gotten around about her engagement to Michael, and it was evident to everyone that this experiment would have more meaning for Maria and Michael than for anyone else concerned. "Michael Harris," she read aloud. The classroom burst into applause, and Maria blushed. Everyone was too busy watching Michael and Maria to notice that Enid was matched up with Ken Matthews, captain of the football team, and Amy Sutton drew

Roger Patman, Bruce's cousin and Olivia's boyfriend.

"Let's get started," Mr. Jaworski said enthusiastically. "Now, each 'husband' has been given a folder with a fact sheet inside it. Girls, why don't you join your classroom 'spouses' now and find out where you live, what you do, and anything else that's in your folder."

"I can't believe this!" Jessica groaned. "Winston's a *bus driver*!"

"What's wrong with that?" Winston asked indignantly. "Consider it a golden chariot, my dear. Besides," he added, looking down at the fact sheet with a smile, "we'll have plenty of room for our seven children."

Jessica looked upset. "And how am I going to have any time for having fun with seven children and a part-time job in a beauty parlor?"

Lila Fowler was examining Bill Chase's folder with horror. "At least your husband has a job," she shrieked. "It looks like I'm doomed to the breadline! Bill's unemployed!"

Elizabeth giggled. She and Bruce sorted through their folder and discovered that Bruce was a doctor and Elizabeth a fourth-grade teacher. They had two children, a boy who was seven years old and a girl who was nine.

Soon everyone had adjusted to his or her new "identity." Olivia and Jeffrey were co-owners of a small metal business. Enid was an actress and Ken Matthews a coach. Amy Sutton was a lawyer and Roger a banker, which seemed to delight Amy. "We've really got it made, Roger," she kept saying. "We'll have to budget all our money for fantastic vacations!"

"What jobs did you two get?" Winston asked Maria and Michael.

Maria laughed. "Michael's a veterinarian, and I'm a housewife," she said. "Can you believe it? I must be the only 'wife' who didn't get a job."

"Being a housewife is a job," Michael pointed out.

Maria rolled her eyes. "I mean a *real* job," she retorted.

"I'll trade with you," Jessica volunteered. "I'd much rather be a housewife than a part-time manicurist, or whatever I am."

"Don't be discontented with your lot, dear," Winston chided her. "Otherwise, you'll start getting all sorts of fancy ideas about things we can't afford. And we can't have that."

Jessica tried to take a swipe at him, but Winston ducked.

"OK, OK, let's get started," Mr. Jaworski announced. "The first part of the unit has to do with family budgeting. Everyone turn to page two of your printout. The number on the top of the page is your annual joint income after taxes. Has everyone found the number?"

"This is impossible," Lila moaned. "Bill, that must be the wrong page number. No one can live on that little money!"

"Now, today's project is to start making a budget. On page three of your printout you'll find several sets of budgetary choices. In part one, for instance, there are several kinds of homes and their monthly rates. Some are higher than others. You will decide where to allocate the money you have. One category will be rental or mortgage allotment. Another is food. Then there's education. And of course, furniture and clothing. And— "

"I think we need to shift our education and rental money to the clothing category," Jessica told Winston. "I'm going to need some new clothes this year, Winston, dear."

"Yeah, then where are we going to live? In the back of the bus?" Winston grumbled.

"You have forty-five minutes," Mr. Jaworski told them. "Don't make any decisions too hastily. You'll have more time to work on your budgets on Wednesday, and then we'll choose a couple to discuss the decisions they've made and why."

Jessica and Elizabeth exchanged amused glances. Clearly the next two weeks were going to be a lot of fun. Jessica could hardly wait to see how Lila Fowler coped with life on unemployment checks.

And it seemed lucky that Maria and Michael had gotten each other. What could be better than for the two of them to pretend at what would soon become the real thing?

Jessica was rushing madly down the crowded hall in school, trying to catch up to Cara Walker and Lila Fowler. "Cara! Lila!" Jessica called as she got closer to the girls. "I've been hoping to find you two together," she added as they turned around with inquisitive smiles.

"What's up?" Cara asked.

"Has Lila told you about her new life as a short-order cook and bride of an unemployed thirty-seven-year-old?" Jessica asked Cara with a giggle.

"Please," Lila said, rolling her eyes. "Don't give me indigestion. I think Mr. Jaworski has really flipped this time."

"Anyway, that isn't why I wanted to catch you. Seeing Michael and Maria together today gave me a great idea. Don't you think we should have a party for them?"

"Like a bridal shower?" Lila asked, her brown eyes widening as she picked a piece of lint off her white skirt. Lila dressed the part of the daughter of one of the richest men in Sweet Valley, and that day she looked especially good. Her white skirt showed her tan off to perfection, and a new perm made her long light brown hair look fuller and prettier than usual.

"No. I mean an engagement party. Something for both of them. I mean, it seems so unfair that they can't even tell their parents. They're probably dying to celebrate. How many times do you get engaged, anyway?"

"You're right, Jess," Lila said thoughtfully. "They really do seem to need some kind of party. Something formal, I think. Something really big and exciting."

"Sounds like a Lila Fowler party!" Cara said and grinned.

Lila snapped her fingers. "What a great idea! We can have it at my place, and it can be a complete surprise!"

Jessica's eyes brightened. "I love surprise parties. When should we have it?"

"How about this Saturday? We'll need a little time to get everything organized, though. We should have really fantastic wedding decorations, silver bells and lots of white everywhere."

"Let's have a wedding cake made!" Jessica exclaimed.

"Shhh," Lila warned her, glancing uneasily

around them. "Remember, it's got to be a secret. Who should we invite?"

Within minutes Jessica and Lila had ticked off the first thirty people who came to mind.

"I don't know, you guys," Cara said anxiously. "Didn't Maria say she and Michael want to keep this really quiet? Maybe having a big party isn't such a good idea."

"Who," Jessica demanded, "said anything about *big*?"

She couldn't see what Cara was fussing about. Michael and Maria clearly needed a party to celebrate their engagement. What could be more natural—and more simple—than inviting a few close friends over for a quiet little celebration in the Fowlers' mansion on the hill?

It was after school before Maria was able to catch up to Winston with the news she had been dreading to break to him. He was on the lawn, doodling in his notebook, when she hurried up to him. "Winston," Maria said nervously, fiddling with the edge of her notebook, "it looks like I might not be able to work with you tomorrow afternoon."

Winston looked down at the ground as the after-school crowd flowed past them. He and Maria had been working every Tuesday and Thursday afternoon for the past few weeks. She had been coaching him on his Student Council campaign. The election was to be held in less than two weeks, and he felt he needed a lot more work. Already Maria had done a great deal. She had helped him make posters for the hallways, had made up hundreds of flyers with his name on them, and had helped pass them out in the hallway. More important, she had given him an enormous amount of moral support. And now, when he needed her most . . .

"Why?" he asked, trying to keep his voice casual.

Maria sighed. "Well, Michael says he needs me to help him pick a present for his older sister. Honestly, I don't see why we have to do it tomorrow afternoon. But—"

"That's OK," Winston said, trying not to show his disappointment. "I understand."

"We can still meet Thursday," Maria said hastily. She couldn't bear the look on Winston's face. It wasn't just his campaign she was thinking about, either. It bothered her to upset him.

The truth was that Maria had come to care a great deal for Winston. They had always been friends, but she used to think he was nothing more than a clown. Like many of her classmates, she had never realized how sensitive he was. She was glad now that she had volunteered to give him a few pointers on his campaign. The hours they had spent together so far had cemented their friendship. She found herself continually impressed with Winston's "other" side. Sure, he was a comedian. He made her laugh so hard somtimes that her sides ached. But that didn't mean he couldn't see the more serious side of life, too.

She hated to let him down now. But Michael had insisted that she break her plans. In fact, they had almost quarreled about it, until Maria backed down and promised to tell Winston she had other plans.

"You sure you can make it then?" Winston asked uncertainly.

"Of course!" Maria assured him.

His face lit up. "That's great," he said with evident relief. "I really want you to hear the revised conclusion I wrote. It's hard for me to tell what it's like. It seems a little naked without a single joke. But I want to know what *you* think. You've got such good judgment, Maria."

Maria felt her face growing warm. Winston had such a peculiar look in his eyes! Almost as though—

She turned away, then spotted Michael bounding toward them, his books under his arm. "Oh, there's Michael," she said, trying to sound natural. "I guess I've got to go now, Winston. So we'll save our meeting for Thursday, OK?"

Michael came up to them, nodded briefly at Winston, then put his arm around Maria and gave her shoulder a squeeze. "Come on, honey," he said. "Let's get going."

Maria swallowed. She wished Michael could be a little nicer to Winston. But she didn't want to upset Michael by saying anything. She walked off arm in arm with Michael, afraid to turn around.

All the same, she knew Winston was watching them. And she felt suddenly confused, as if something had happened that she couldn't quite bring herself to understand.

Four

"Elizabeth," Jessica said dreamily, her hands folded behind her neck as she watched the lone fluffy cloud floating across the clear sky, "do you think you and Jeffrey will end up getting married?"

It was Tuesday afternoon, and Elizabeth was doing her homework on the patio surrounding the Wakefields' swimming pool while her sister lazed on the diving board. Now she looked up from her math problems and studied her twin. "Jeffrey and I don't even know what movie we're going to see this weekend, let alone what we'll be doing months from now. How could we possibly guess about the future?"

"What I mean is," Jessica said stubbornly, "do you think he's the sort of guy you could imagine being married to?"

Elizabeth chewed the end of her pencil reflectively. "Isn't it strange," she said. "I don't think you and I have ever talked about the sort of man we'd imagine as a husband."

"Well, I sure hope I don't end up marrying Winston Egbert in real life," Jessica said moodily. "Not to mention having to fight over clothing budgets. Winston claims I only get fifty dollars a year to cover everything!"

Elizabeth laughed. "At the rate you're going, I bet you'll never settle down and get married. You can't even go out with the same guy two weekends in a row!"

Jessica pretended to look hurt. "You think I'm going to be a spinster, don't you?" she complained.

"Oh, I don't know," Elizabeth said playfully. "Maybe someday you'll find someone crazy enough to put up with you." She ducked as her sister threw a towel at her. "But seriously," she said, "I think Jaworski's project is a good one. I know you think Maria and Michael's engagement is the world's most romantic event, but I guess I think of marriage as something bigger than romance. I mean, think about it, Jess. Imagine spending the rest of your life with someone!"

Jessica looked pained. "I can't," she admitted. A sudden pang seemed to strike her. "You don't think I'll end up an old maid, do you?" she asked. "So far I haven't been very good at long-term relationships. *You're* the one who's good at that."

But Elizabeth wasn't listening to Jessica. "I think I just heard a car stop in our driveway."

Jessica sat up and swung her legs over the diving board. "Oh, that must be Lila. She wants my advice about the party we're throwing for Maria and Michael."

"Party?" Elizabeth said blankly. "What party?"

"The surprise party we're giving them to celebrate their engagement, silly," Jessica said airily. She leaped nimbly off the diving board onto the soft ground. "I've got to go let her in."

"Will you bring Prince Albert out when you come? The poor thing has been in the house all day," Elizabeth called after her twin. She didn't want to nag Jessica, but even though the puppy was supposed to be chiefly her twin's responsibility, Elizabeth could tell that she herself was going to have to do more than her share to look after his welfare.

A few minutes later Jessica re-emerged from the house, a bouncing Prince Albert on the leash Elizabeth had bought him. Lila was trailing behind, her nose wrinkling at the sight of the puppy.

"I know I said I thought Prince Albert was really cute and everything, but you know, he seems to be getting spoiled," she complained, sitting carefully on a patio chair and smoothing her skirt over her knees. "Don't let him jump on me. If he gets hair or anything on this new skirt, I'll *kill* him."

Elizabeth couldn't suppress a twinge of pleasure when Prince Albert jumped up to greet the newcomer. A bit of dirt got onto Lila's skirt, and she looked as if she were ready to kill. Elizabeth didn't like Lila Fowler very much. She found her spoiled and affected, and she was secretly proud of Prince Albert, though she pretended to scold him.

"I could really start to hate this animal," Lila said. "I hope you plan on sending him to obedience school. He is acting like a mongrel."

"Lila," Jessica said warningly, throwing her arms around the puppy and giving his golden head an exuberant kiss, "you're going to have to get used to Princie. He's here to stay."

"Well, at least he's named for royalty," Lila said, resigned. "Anyway, I didn't come over to talk canines. I've got to find out what you think of the plans for the party."

Elizabeth twirled a lock of her blond hair around her index finger. "I hate to intrude," she said dryly, "but don't you think it's a little inappropriate to have a surprise party for Maria and Michael when they've made it clear that their engagement is secret?"

"You sound like Cara," Lila said, miffed. "What's the big deal? The party's a secret. The engagement's a secret. What could be more secret? Honestly!"

Jessica giggled. "Lila's right, Liz," she said. "We're not stupid. We're not inviting the Harrises or the Santellis, after all."

"Is it going to be a small party?" Elizabeth asked.

Lila said "yes" and Jessica said "no" at the same instant, and each stared accusingly at the other.

"How many people?" Elizabeth tried again.

"Fifty," they repeated in unison. This time they started laughing, and Prince Albert, trying to get in on the fun, jumped up to lick Lila's face.

"Get this mutt *away* from me!" Lila shrieked. "Anyway, Jess, I've got to ask you what you think of the engagement present I cooked up. What do you think of arranging for them to be on the 'Newlywed Game'?"

"Isn't that a little premature?" Elizabeth asked wryly.

Lila looked hurt. "They're going to get married soon, aren't they?" she demanded.

Jessica looked thoughtful. "Actually, Maria never said. I wonder when they *are* getting married."

41

Elizabeth didn't say anything else. She listened to her sister and Lila enthusiastically discuss decorations, music, food, and the guest list. She assumed they were including her on the list, but she didn't want to go.

It seemed to Elizabeth that a party this size didn't stand much chance of staying secret for long. She didn't want any part of it. Because the more people who found out about the party, the greater the chance someone would reveal Michael and Maria's secret.

Elizabeth didn't want to butt in and warn the couple about the party. She knew her sister would kill her if she did. But she decided then and there that she wanted no part of it. It seemed far too big a risk to take.

And there was no telling what would happen if either the Harrises or the Santellis learned the truth about Michael and Maria.

Maria and Michael were coming out of the Valley Mall together, the package with the gift they had selected tucked under Michael's arm. "I think Kate's really going to like the scarf," Maria said, tucking her arm through Michael's.

"I hope so," he said. "She's kind of hard to please sometimes."

Maria didn't respond. Secretly she thought "hard to please" was an understatement. From everything Michael had told her, it sounded as though Kate was pretty hard to get along with at times. But she didn't want to start on their families. Everything was perfect between her and Michael—except for one thing: families.

"When are you going to give it to her?" she asked him as they crossed the parking lot to his car.

"Probably tomorrow night. We're having a big birthday dinner for her. She's going to be coming to my match on Thursday, so we'll have to be careful. Remember to take off the ring," he told her.

Maria's face clouded over. "Thursday? You have a tennis match on Thursday? I thought it was on Saturday."

"It was, but it got changed." Michael frowned. "You're going to be there, aren't you? You know how much it means to me when you come to my matches."

Maria bit her lip. "Well, the thing is, Michael, I promised Winston I'd help him with his campaign speech on Thursday afternoon. After today I really don't think I can just say no to him again. Maybe—"

"You've been helping Winston for weeks!" Michael cut in angrily. "How much time can it take to prepare a stupid campaign speech?

You'd think he was running for president or something!"

Maria's eyes flashed. She had to fight hard to retain her composure. "It really isn't like you, Michael. You're being so possessive," she objected. "I mean, you've never acted like this before!"

Michael turned pale. "That isn't really fair of you to say. I'm *not* being possessive. It's just that I want you to be there on Thursday. Come on, Maria," he pleaded, putting his arm around her and pulling her close to him. "I need you more than Winston does."

Maria felt her heartbeat quicken. She loved Michael so much! And she didn't want to argue with him. It made her feel terrible.

On the other hand, she was used to her independence. Michael had never been like this before. They each had their share of activities. In fact, they were both really busy, and they had always been respectful of each other's decisions.

That was one of the things that had made Maria fall in love with Michael in the first place. Before Michael, she had never really cared for a guy. Not in any serious way. She'd had a few dates, but nothing important. From the very start, she had sensed Michael was different. He was so intelligent! She felt that she could talk about anything in the world with him and he would understand.

She fell in love with Michael almost as soon as they started dating. But both of them knew their parents would be furious if they found out about Michael and Maria's relationship. And it was all because of that fight over the Henderson contract. The feud was so old now, Maria wasn't sure she understood it entirely—or that either her father or Michael's father did, either. What had happened was this: Mr. Henderson was an old client. When Maria's father discovered he was a dishonest businessman, he dropped his account without consulting Michael's father first. Michael's father accused Mr. Santelli of dealing behind his back. Both became enraged, and within weeks their partnership was dissolved.

Michael and Maria had suffered as a result of their parents' enmity. They both cared very much about their families, and it hurt them to sneak around behind their backs now. But they were madly in love.

The engagement had been Michael's idea. He had often talked about it before he actually gave Maria the ring. He felt he couldn't keep on lying to his parents, constantly deceiving them. He told Maria he thought the best way would be to make a step that would let their parents know how serious they were about each other.

The plan was to choose a time and tell both sets of parents the truth—that they had fallen deeply in love and were engaged. There would be no splitting them once their parents saw the ring.

But ever since they had become engaged, Michael had said nothing about broaching the subject with their parents. In fact, he seemed even more insistent that they keep their relationship a secret. It puzzled Maria, and it hurt her a little, too. She didn't want to have to keep lying.

"Michael," she said softly, "don't you think it's time to talk to your parents? And to mine? I thought that was the plan. We can't keep our engagement secret forever."

Michael looked pale. "That is the plan," he assured her. "But I don't think it's a very good time right now. My father's been under so much stress at work. And my mom isn't feeling well."

Maria sighed. She thought Michael's mother was a hypochondriac. If they had to wait until she was feeling well, Maria thought, their engagement would be a secret forever! "Let's not fight, anyway," she said, resigned. "I can't stand arguing with you." *It reminds me of what I remember about Kate and Richard*, she thought miserably. *Unhappy and stuck with each other.*

"Promise you'll come see me play Thursday," Michael said in a soft voice, kissing her forehead tenderly. "You know you give me good luck."

"Well," Maria said wearily, "I guess I can tell Winston I'm busy again. But his campaign is almost over. The election is coming up. If I could find someone else to take over for me . . ."

"That's a great idea!" Michael exclaimed. "I'm sure there are a lot of people who would do a good job."

Maria still felt uneasy about the situation. "All right, I'll be at the tennis match," she said with a sigh.

"Good," Michael said happily, giving her a warm hug. "To tell you the truth, Winston's been bugging me lately. I don't like the way he looks at you."

Maria reddened. "What's that supposed to mean?" she asked.

"I don't know. I just don't like it, that's all."

Maria wanted to say something in Winston's defense, but suddenly she had an overwhelming desire to drop the subject. She didn't want to talk about Winston Egbert. It was dumb to be so disappointed about Thursday anyway, she thought. What was the big deal about helping Winston with a silly campaign speech?

Michael was right, she assured herself, tucking her arm through his again. Winston was making too much out of the whole thing. There was no point in letting him get too dependent on her anyway.

Not now. She was engaged—practically a married woman! Which meant Michael was right to demand more of her time.

She felt terrible about their argument. It was the first disagreement they'd had since they'd gotten engaged. And she was determined it would be the last.

Five

Maria couldn't believe how upset she felt Wednesday afternoon. This was the moment she had been dreading—the moment when she had to break it to Winston that she couldn't manage his campaign anymore. She hurried across the lawn to find him in his usual spot, relaxing under a big shade tree in front of the school. Stopping in front of him, Maria took a deep breath, put her knapsack down, and said, "Winston, I don't think I'm going to be able to work with you on your campaign anymore. I feel absolutely rotten about the whole thing. I mean, I know I promised, but"—her voice dropped off—"something's come up," she finished hastily. She knew that sounded lame, but she wasn't sure of what to say. The thought of saying that she had promised to watch Michael play tennis was out of the question. She knew Winston would think she wasn't being a good friend. After all, she had made a deal with him. She had promised to see him through his campaign, and here she was, abandoning him just when he needed moral support most!

Winston ran his fingers through his short dark hair. He looked flushed and distraught and swallowed once or twice, as if fighting for control. "Maria, did I say something wrong last week? Did I do anything to upset you?"

Maria fidgeted nervously. She wasn't used to hearing Winston sound so serious. "Of course not," she said, feeling terrible. "It's just—well, I've decided to start piano lessons up again, and the only time Mrs. Haywood can take me is on Tuesday and Thursday afternoons. So between the lessons and cheerleading practice, I'm just too busy." She took a deep breath. "You really don't need me anyway," she assured him. "You're guaranteed to win the election. You've been doing such a great job."

"Sure, sure," Winston said, sighing. His face was beginning to resume it's usual good-humored expression. "You realize, don't you, that you're breaking my heart."

Maria stared at him. "Quit kidding around," she said uneasily.

Winston grabbed at his heart, pretending to fall over. "Who's kidding?" he cried with mock anguish. "She's killing me," he gasped to Olivia Davidson, who was passing by.

"Winston stop it," Maria begged him. Other people sitting on the lawn were staring at them, and she was embarrassed. Embarrassed and confused. Why did he have to make a joke out of everything? If he really minded so much that she couldn't help him anymore, wouldn't he act genuinely upset instead of clowning around? She didn't know what to think. Then she began to giggle despite herself. Winston was always able to get a laugh out of her. She was going to miss working with him, she realized.

"Listen, Winston, I've been thinking. Maybe I can make up for abandoning you in your hour of need by finding someone who can take my place."

Winston covered his ears. "No one can take your place," he said passionately.

Maria giggled again. "I'm being serious now, Winston."

"So am I!" Winston said, sinking to one knee and taking her hand in his. "Without you, madam, my sun won't shine. My days will be night. My—"

"Winston," Maria cut in, shaking her head at him and smiling, "if you don't stop fooling around, I'll never be able to help you."

Winston sighed and stood up again. "The

age of romance has vanished forever," he said gloomily. "Go on, Maria. I'm all ears."

Maria stared at him. The trouble with Winston was that it was impossible to tell what was really going on in that goofy mind of his! "I feel bad," she told him. "I'd like to find someone to take my place for the next week. Have you got any suggestions?"

"No," Winston said sadly. "I don't."

"Well, I'll think about it," Maria assured him. Spotting Michael, she grabbed her knapsack and swung it over her shoulder. Something told her it would be best to end her conversation with Winston now.

It was bad enough having to quit on someone she liked so much. But the thought of another quarrel with Michael was more than she could bear.

"Winston, is anything the matter?" Elizabeth asked, staring at the uneaten food on the tray he had pushed to one side. It was Thursday, and she was eating lunch with Winston at one of the patio tables outside the cafeteria. But Winston, who usually had an astonishing appetite considering how thin he was, had barely taken a bite of his food. It was hard to believe that this was the same boy who had once tried to break the world's pizza-eating record.

"I'm fine," he said moodily. "Just fine."

Elizabeth gave him a look. "You don't sound like yourself," she remarked. "You're sure nothing's wrong?"

"I'm just worried about the campaign for Student Council PTA rep. The election is a week from tomorrow, and I feel like I'm not getting anywhere. Maria was helping me, but now she's too busy. She says she's starting piano lessons or something. . . ." His voice trailed off unhappily.

"Well, Maria must have a lot on her mind these days," Elizabeth pointed out. "I'm sure she wouldn't tell you she was too busy unless she really was."

Winston looked grieved. "I don't think Michael likes me very much. He always gives me dirty looks when we run into each other."

Elizabeth raised her eyebrows, surprised. "Why wouldn't Michael like you?" she asked. "I didn't think you two knew each other very well."

"We don't. But I still get the feeling . . . I don't know . . . that he thinks I'm trying to—you know, take Maria away from him or something."

Elizabeth's eyes widened. She took a long look at Winston. She knew him well enough to suspect he was genuinely upset about something, and she was determined to get to the bottom of it. "Winston," she said carefully, "you don't have sort of a crush on Maria, do you?"

Winston turned beet red. "Of course not! She's practically married."

"I know," Elizabeth said, smiling. "But that doesn't mean she isn't a likable girl."

"She's more than likable," Winston gushed. "She's so sweet—and so pretty! Every time I'm with her I think—" He broke off in midsentence, obviously embarrassed.

"Don't worry. I'll keep your secret," Elizabeth said gently. "I don't blame you for liking her, Winston. She seems like a really nice person."

Winston's face showed genuine misery. "What am I going to do?" he cried. "Liz, I think about her all the time! I like her so much it hurts. You know what I mean?"

Elizabeth nodded sympathetically.

"But there's no way I can let her know. I thought about it before. I was even dumb enough to think she kind of liked me, too. And then she goes and gets *engaged*." Winston looked bitter. "So I guess that's it. No wonder Michael doesn't like me," he added unhappily. "I don't blame him. I must be a real jerk, falling in love with a girl who's practically married!"

"Well," Elizabeth said philosophically, "if it

makes you feel any better, I don't think what you feel is one bit wrong. I think it's only natural."

"Thanks," Winston said sadly. "But even if it isn't wrong, it's hopeless. There's no way I can ever let Maria know how I feel. Face it, Liz, it's a no-win situation."

Elizabeth didn't know what to say to comfort him. She had to agree with him—the situation seemed absolutely hopeless.

"Liz! The phone's for you!" Jessica called, sticking her head inside the door to her sister's bedroom. "Try not to take too long. I promised Lila I'd call her at nine."

"I'll do my best," Elizabeth said dryly as she reached for the receiver. She couldn't believe how proprietary her sister could be about the telephone sometimes! It seemed especially funny to be reminded about not taking too long from a twin who could manage to talk on the telephone until she was hoarse. But as usual Elizabeth couldn't be annoyed with her sister for long. She was even smiling as she said "hello" into the receiver.

To her surprise, it wasn't Jeffrey on the line. An unfamiliar female voice said "Liz? Have you got a minute to talk?"

"Sure," Elizabeth said, trying to place the voice.

"It's Maria, Maria Santelli. I hope I'm not bothering you or anything."

"No, of course not," Elizabeth said, her curiosity piqued. Why was Maria calling her? She tucked her feet up underneath her on the bed, waiting to hear what Maria had to say.

"Listen, Liz, I know you must be wondering why I'm calling. The truth is, I saw you having lunch with Winston today, and it gave me an idea. You and Winston are good friends, aren't you?"

"Yes," Elizabeth said slowly. "We've known each other for ages." She could feel her guard go up. She hoped Maria wasn't going to ask her anything that might cause her to betray Winston's confidence. She had assured him that his secret was safe with her, and she would never go back on a promise.

But Maria seemed to have something else on her mind. "You know I've been helping Winston with his campaign for Student Council, right?"

"Yes, he told me something about it," Elizabeth said casually.

"Well, I can't help him out anymore. I told him it was because I started piano lessons again, but the truth is Michael just can't stand my spending so much time with Winston." She sighed heavily. "Crazy as it may seem, I think Michael's a little jealous."

"It doesn't seem that crazy," Elizabeth said.

Encouraged, Maria continued. "See, Michael's changed about things like this since we got engaged. I guess it really changes the way a couple behaves."

"I don't see why it should," Elizabeth told her. She didn't add the thought that occurred to her, that Michael's possessiveness and jealousy seemed to be a strong signal that all wasn't well with the couple, engaged or not.

"Oh, you wouldn't understand," Maria said quickly. "You and Jeffrey haven't known each other all that long. And you two don't have a real commitment to each other yet."

"That's true," Elizabeth said, secretly annoyed. She shifted uncomfortably on her bed. "I'm not sure I really understand about Winston, but I guess it really isn't my business. It's between you and Michael."

"Yes," Maria said. "I didn't want to bother you, but when I talked to Winston, I told him I'd try to think of someone who might be able to take my place—you know, help him out with his speech, kind of give him some moral support between now and next Friday. The thing is, I couldn't think of anyone. Winston is touchy about this. It's the first time he's really ever done anything in public that isn't a comedy routine. When I saw you two having lunch today, it was like a light bulb going off. You'd be absolutely *perfect*, Liz. I know Winston would be happy, and—"

"Maria," Elizabeth interrupted, "if Winston wanted me to help him, wouldn't he ask me himself?"

Maria sounded offended. "He's probably too shy," she answered. "Don't feel you have to answer right away," she added quickly. "Maybe you could think it over and let me know tomorrow."

"I think I can let you know right now," Elizabeth said, trying not to let her impatience show. She didn't like the way Maria sounded at all. It seemed irresponsible to Elizabeth for Maria to have quit on Winston, and inappropriate to try to arrange a substitute without letting Winston think or act for himself. "In the first place, I'm way too busy to do anything for the next week. I'm helping Jeffrey with a special photo insert for *The Oracle*, and I've got tons of homework. I really don't have time to take on anything else for the next few weeks."

"You said 'in the first place,' " Maria pressed her. "Does this mean you have another reason, besides being too busy?"

Elizabeth hesitated for a moment, then said, "Well, I just don't think I should get involved. You and Winston had an agreement. It seems to me that you owe it to him to follow through."

Maria was silent for a minute. "You just don't understand," she said softly. For a minute it sounded as if she were about to cry, but the next minute her voice turned cold and angry. "You just don't know what it's like being engaged," she said accusingly. "In fact, I don't think you're trying to understand. I bet you're jealous of Michael and me."

"Jealous?" Elizabeth said incredulously. "Why would I be jealous?"

Maria was close to tears. "You're jealous because we're engaged!" she cried. And before Elizabeth could respond, Maria had slammed the phone down.

"Wow," Elizabeth said, shaking her head. She was about to call Jeffrey to tell him what had happened when Jessica opened the door.

"Are you done yet? I want to call Lila and see how the party's coming," Jessica announced.

"Jess, I don't think this party is a very good idea," Elizabeth said, putting the receiver back on the hook. She gave Jessica a rundown of what had just transpired. "Something must be brewing with those two. It doesn't sound to me like they're really stable and happy right now."

Jessica waved her hand dismissively. "It's just jitters," she said. "An engagement party is just what Maria needs to calm her down."

Elizabeth opened her mouth to object, but it was too late. Jessica had walked out of the room, closing the door behind her. Clearly Jessica had no intention of suggesting that Lila cancel the party. It figured, Elizabeth thought. For those two nothing short of a disaster could threaten a party once it had been planned.

She just hoped that whatever happened, Michael and Maria would be able to avoid a disaster!

Six

Maria examined herself critically in the mirror in the girls' bathroom. It was strange, she thought, that she didn't look any different since she and Michael had gotten engaged. It seemed to be the sort of thing that ought to be written all over one's face. Such a momentous change . . .

She fumbled through her pocketbook for the tiny jewelry box where she kept Michael's ring until she got to school each day. It still made her nervous, slipping the ring on her finger. She held the left hand up, admiring the perfect diamond. It was so beautiful! If only she could wear it all the time, especially since Michael had gone to so much trouble getting it for her. When she thought of all those hours he had put in, working as a part-time mechanic at the filling station to earn the money for it, it made her feel like crying. She wished she could wear the ring all the time so everyone would know the truth about them. That was what she really wanted, for everything to be out in the open, once and for all.

But there was no point in thinking that way. Maria felt ashamed of herself for her behavior lately. She really hadn't been acting like herself. Take the way she had blown up at Elizabeth Wakefield the night before. That wasn't something she would have done ever before! The pressure of the secret engagement was making her much jumpier than she had ever been—and more defensive. She would have to apologize to Elizabeth. And to Winston, too.

Maria had given the matter a great deal of thought after she'd hung up on Elizabeth. She hadn't been able to fall asleep, and she had had plenty of time to go over and over the events of the past few weeks.

She didn't like her own behavior. Perhaps Elizabeth had been too forthright in suggesting that she shouldn't quit on Winston, but wasn't she right? The truth was that Maria had made a commitment to Winston. Not as big a commitment as the one she and Michael had made, but a commitment nonetheless. She owed it to him to follow through with it. She was going to tell him so—right after she found Michael and told him that nothing was going to interfere with her helping Winston out next Tuesday and Thursday afternoons.

Michael was going to have to understand. And why shouldn't he? He had always been reasonable about her decisions. Why should that change now that they had decided to spend the rest of their lives together?

"The rest of our lives," Maria murmured.

The phrase didn't seem quite as exciting as it had a few weeks before, when Michael had murmured it to her by Secca Lake. Now it seemed bigger—more solemn.

Maybe even a little bit frightening.

Mr. Jaworski cleared his throat loudly as he surveyed the high-spirited group before him. "Today," Mr. Jaworski said, "we're going to finish our budget unit and move on to special problem solving. What I'm going to do now is ask you to turn to page eight of your printouts. Here you'll find a 'problem' of some sort, ranging from a crisis, such as your home being ruined by a fire or flood, to an emotional problem—the death of a relative, for example, or a difficult family issue, such as sibling rivalry among your children. After you've finished balancing your budget, I want you to read through your problem case and discuss it with your partner for half an hour. Then I'm going to call on two couples to present their discussions to the class. One couple will describe their budget, tell us how they arrived at it and what difficulties they encounterd in their discussions. The second couple will present a tentative solution to the problem they've been presented with."

Jessica groaned. "It figures. We *would* be the couple whose house gets wrecked. Winston, why can't we just have something nice and simple like problem children?"

"Now get to work," Mr. Jaworski chided. "I want you all to be ready when it's time to make your presentations."

For the next half hour the partners worked together, lively discussions ensuing as they faced the "problems" they found in their folders and settled on their family budgets. Most pairs joked and laughed as they arrived at tentative solutions. But Maria and Michael were taking the whole thing with deadly seriousness.

"I still don't think we've got this budget right," Maria objected. "But I guess we can't do any better than this, since we've only got your salary to work with. If I had a job, we'd be able to afford summer camp for the kids."

"Who needs summer camp?" Michael scoffed.

"Anyway, I'm glad you don't have a job. Otherwise, who'd be around to take care of the kids?"

"Michael, you can't be serious," Maria said, staring at him. "Nobody talks that way anymore!"

"Nobody—except Michael Harris," he said. "I don't want my wife to have to work! I want her to be able to stay at home and take care of my kids. Like in the good old days."

"I hope you're kidding," she said with more vehemence than she had planned. "There's no way I'm going to spend my whole life hanging around the house."

Michael was irritated. "What's the matter with you lately? You can't take a joke anymore. Why are you always so tense?"

Maria looked away from him. "I guess you're right. I am a little tense," she admitted. "Let's leave our budget the way it is and look at the 'problem' we were assigned."

"OK. Here it is: 'Your twelve-year-old son is in bad trouble. He's been caught shoplifting twice, and the police have threatened to send him to a home for juvenile delinquents if he's apprehended again. You've consulted a psychologist who has suggested family therapy. What will you do?'"

"Oh, no," Maria moaned. "I wish we'd gotten something easy, like our house burning down."

"Well, this doesn't seem very hard to me. There's no point messing around with psychologists. Anyway, we can't afford it. We didn't factor it into our budget. So we just tell the kid to get in line, or else. And I'll see to it he doesn't do it again, whatever it takes."

Maria's eyes widened. "You don't mean you'd hit him, do you?"

"Why not? It sounds like he needs it."

Maria looked horrified. "You're not going to hit our son, Michael. He obviously needs a psychologist. Your attitude is probably the reason he's doing this in the first place. Can't you see this is just a cry for help?"

"That's dumb," Michael said. "I don't believe that sort of stuff. It's all pop psychology."

"Well, *I'm* going to go to the psychologist with him," Maria said, glaring. "You can do what you like."

"Maria," Michael said, putting his hand over hers. Her voice had been a little loud, and a few of their classmates were turning to stare. "You're taking this way too seriously. It's only a game!"

Maria picked nervously at the edge of her

notebook. "I don't think it's just a game. I think it's serious."

Michael was about to respond when Mr. Jaworski stood up and cleared his throat. "Time to share your results with the rest of us!" he declared. "Let's have a presentation of a family budget first. Jessica and Winston, why don't you tell us how you've allocated your salaries?"

Jessica and Winston stood up, exchanged glances, and walked agreeably to the front of the room. "We seem to have a few problems with our budget," Winston admitted. "I earn seventeen thousand dollars a year, and Jessica —my dear wife—earns six thousand dollars. We have seven children, which seems to be a problem. We've opted to live in a rental apartment, which has four bedrooms, because we can't afford to buy a house."

"I don't think owning a house is very important, either," Jessica chimed in. "However, I've convinced my husband to let me have half my yearly salary for clothing and entertainment."

The group burst into laughter at this. "Can anyone see any difficulties yet with this budget?" Mr. Jaworski asked. Soon everyone was chiming in with ideas.

Maria didn't find it very funny. In fact she was the only one in the group who wasn't having fun. The situation struck her as very serious. Who ever thought about things like budgets or problem children when they talked about getting married? She and Michael didn't even have real jobs. They were too young, and they still had to finish school. Would they have to ask his parents for money? Hers wouldn't want to help them, not if she were marrying Michael Harris. They wouldn't want her getting married at this age anyway. They wanted her to finish school and go to college—and she had always wanted that, too. What had convinced Michael and her that this was a good time to get married?

To Maria's dismay, Winston and Jessica were sitting down, and Mr. Jaworski was calling on Michael and her to present their discussion of the problem they had been given. Maria felt her face turn red with embarrassment. The last thing she wanted to do was to talk about imaginary problems in front of the class. Still, she had no choice. She went to the front of the room with Michael, but she let him do all the talking. She barely listened to his terse description of their decision to use "firmer discipline" rather than therapy to keep their son in line.

She didn't want to think about imaginary problems anymore. It seemed that she and Michael had enough real problems to keep them busy without resorting to make-believe.

*   *   *

Michael and Maria strolled out of school together, deep in discussion about Winston. Maria couldn't believe her ears. It sounded as if Michael were finally coming around to seeing things from her point of view! Relief washed over her as he put his arm around her. "Well, I don't really see why it's so important to you. But if it is, then go ahead and help him," Michael said, although his tone was a little sulky.

Maria felt an incredible sense of relief. "Michael Harris, I love you!" she shrieked, throwing her arms around his neck. Now that he had consented, she realized how much she really cared about helping Winston. The whole world looked much brighter than it had that morning.

"I don't like it, though," Michael reminded her as they stood on the lawn. But Maria wasn't listening. She could barely wait to find Winston and tell him the good news. "There he is!" she exclaimed, spotting Winston coming out of the main doors. She hurried over to meet him.

"Guess what?" she said, giving him a big smile.

"I'm awful at guessing," Winston said. She thought he looked happy to see her, but it was hard to tell.

"Are you willing to give me another chance

next week? I want to sign up again as your number-one fan and supporter, and one hundred percent of your campaign work force," Maria told him, her eyes shining.

Winston's face lit up. "You mean it? You really still want to help?"

"I really still want to help," she assured him.

"But what about the piano lessons?"

"Oh, those can wait a couple weeks more," Maria said quickly. "Anyway, your election is more important." She lowered her eyes shyly. "I'm just glad you're still willing to let me help."

Winston looked overjoyed. "But—" He stared past her at Michael. "Michael doesn't mind?"

Maria reddened. Had he guessed the real reason why she had been forced to cancel on him this past week? "Of course not," she said quickly.

She knew Michael was watching them, and she knew that she was going to have to listen to his complaints and objections when she went back to him.

For the first time, Maria found herself wondering if she and Michael were right for each other. Was it normal for them to be fighting so much? Why couldn't things just be fun and uncomplicated again, the way they were with Winston?

Ashamed of her disloyal thoughts, Maria excused herself and headed back to the spot where Michael was waiting for her.

The whole weekend was looming in front of them. She just wished she were looking forward to it. She didn't seem to enjoy anything anymore. Everything seemed so complicated, so difficult. It had been this way for a while now. Ever since she and Michael had gotten engaged.

"OK, they're coming!" Lila exclaimed, jumping up from her perch. Lila, Jessica, and Cara had been sitting out under the umbrellas on the terrace next to the cafeteria, waiting for Michael and Maria to pass by. It was the moment they had been waiting for all week.

"You really think they're going to buy this thing about coming over to see Christopher?" Cara asked dubiously.

Lila gave her a murderous look. "Christopher," she said imperiously, "happens to be my very favorite cousin, Cara Walker. Why wouldn't they jump at the chance to come over for a little party I'm throwing in his honor?"

Jessica giggled. "Lila has a point," she reminded Cara. "And something about the way she puts it makes it all seem so much more *important* than any of us might have realized, don't you think?"

71

She and Cara both laughed. There was nothing funnier than Lila when she was trying hard to be serious, as she was right now. But then Lila took parties very seriously, especially when she was giving them or when the party was a surprise.

The girls had decided the best plan was to find a way to get Maria and Michael over to Lila's the following night. They needed some pretense that was important enough so the couple wouldn't refuse, but casual enough to make the real event a wonderful surprise. Lila was the one who thought of Christopher, her handsome older cousin who lived in Kennebunkport, Maine. Since Christopher had come out to visit several months earlier, Lila had often spoken of him to her friends. It seemed a perfect pretext.

Lila went up to the pair. "Maria! Michael!" she purred. "What a lucky coincidence that I ran into you!"

"What's up, Lila?" Maria asked pleasantly.

Lila beamed. "I was just wondering," she said in a honeyed voice, "if you two have any plans for tomorrow night. Because if you don't," she added hastily, not giving them a chance to respond, "you *have* to come over to my place. My cousin Christopher is coming back to town, and I'm having a few people over to welcome

72

him back to Sweet Valley. He's just *dying* to see you both again," she added emphatically.

Maria and Michael exchanged glances. "Uh, we don't have any plans, as a matter of fact," Maria admitted. "I don't really remember that Christopher had a chance to get to know us all that well, but—"

"Of course he did!" Lila shrieked. "What are you saying? He's spoken of nothing but you two ever since I told him—you know," she added, dropping her voice, "about your *engagement*."

Jessica came up beside Lila, said hello to Michael and Maria, then nudged Lila sharply in the ribs, clearly signaling that Lila was getting dangerously close to giving away the real reason for the next night's get-together. Lila gave Jessica a dirty look. "What I mean is that he really *does* want to see you both again. He thought you were both so sweet."

"Well, that sounds great, Lila," Michael said uncertainly. "What time should we come over?"

"Eight," Lila said. "Eight o'clock on the dot. After that the servants get really grumpy, and besides, we might take Christopher out to a movie or something. So be sure to be there *right on time*."

Michael and Maria assured Lila they would be on time and then strolled off together toward the parking lot. Lila turned back to Jessica and Cara only to find them doubled up with laughter. "What's wrong?" she demanded, looking upset. "What in the world are you two laughing at?"

Jessica wiped tears of merriment from her eyes. "Do you think you could have made the whole thing any more obvious?"

"Eight o'clock," Cara mimicked her. "Because otherwise we might miss a very important something-or-other. Or the servants might turn into pumpkins." She and Jessica began to laugh again.

"Cut it out, you two," Lila said, miffed. "'I think I did a really good job. I'm sure they have no idea anything's up."

Jessica shook her head. "Well, I think you're right. I think they didn't guess a thing. But I don't think you deserve much of the credit for that, Lila. I think they're just too wrapped up in each other to suspect anything."

Lila wrinkled her nose. "You two just don't know anything about etiquette," she said imperiously, sweeping past them toward the parking lot. "You just don't know how to invite people to anything." She gave them a haughty look over her shoulder.

But Jessica and Cara were laughing too hard to pay any attention. Granted, neither Michael nor Maria had seemed to suspect anything. But Jessica and Cara still found Lila's attempt to be casual uproarious.

"If this is any indication of how things are going to be, tomorrow night should be a riot!" Cara said, grinning.

Jessica agreed. She could hardly wait for the party. She was convinced that despite Lila's poor theatrics, the couple really was going to be surprised.

In fact, they were probably going to receive the surprise of their lives!

Seven

"I can't wait for the party tonight!" Jessica declared, running a hairbrush through her silky hair. "What do you think of my hair this way, Liz? Do you think I should get a perm?" Jessica had set her naturally wavy blond hair so that it was very full and curly.

Elizabeth shot her a look. "You remember what happened the last time you tried to do something drastic to your appearance," she said reprovingly. She was referring to the time a short while before when Jessica, tired of being an identical twin, had dyed her hair black, changed her style of dressing, and assumed an entirely new personality. Ironically, she had almost lost a modeling assignment she had been trying for as a result.

Jessica looked pained at the recollection.

"Maybe you're right. Anyway *Vogue* says permed hair is going out of style."

Elizabeth looked at the cream-colored dress she had selected for Lila's party. "I still think this whole thing is wrong," she said unhappily. "If Jeffrey weren't so big on going, I wouldn't be in on it at all."

"Jeffrey has a lot of sense," Jessica said serenely, applying some eyeliner to deepen the color of her blue-green eyes. "This party's going to be fabulous! You should see the Fowlers' place. It looks like something out of *Bride's* magazine."

"Well, I still think it's a bad idea. For one thing, both the Harrises and Santellis could easily find out. And that would be a disaster."

"How could they find out? It's going to be a complete surprise." Jessica giggled. "I think Lila's idea to tell Maria and Michael to come by to see her cousin Christopher is perfect. Who'd ever suspect we'll all be there, hiding?"

"Well, I just hope it goes smoothly," Elizabeth said, frowning. "If it doesn't—"

"Don't be such a worrywart," Jessica chided her. "I wish I could have bought that silver dress I saw in Lisette's," she added sorrowfully. "It was gorgeous! It would've been perfect for tonight. This old thing," she added disparagingly, picking up the hem of her aquamarine halter dress, "has really had it. Do you think Mom and Dad would be willing to consider giving us more of an allowance?"

"No chance," Elizabeth said. "You know Mom. She'll tell you to get a part-time job. Like the one you had in the dating agency," she added with a giggle. Jessica had gotten into some real scrapes, but her job at the computer dating agency had always struck Elizabeth as one of the funniest. Jessica had decided after a short while that she was such a pro that she could dip into the company's files to find the perfect woman for the twins' older brother, Steven. None of the women Jessica had "found" for him had been the least bit appropriate. Jessica gave up the job after she tried to fix herself up and chose a real dud. That had been one of her last money-making schemes, and she had been burned badly enough to try to get along with only her allowance for months since!

Jessica frowned at her reflection. If only she had as much money as Lila did! Lila could have bought that silver dress without even batting an eyelid.

But there wasn't time to worry about it now. They were supposed to be at the Fowlers' in half an hour. And for everything to work the way it was supposed to, they had to be there right on time!

*   *   *

"You sure look nice tonight," Michael said huskily as Maria got into his car. He took her in his arms and gave her a long, lingering kiss.

Maria returned the embrace half-heartedly. She had been waiting for Michael in the usual spot, two blocks from her house. But that night he had been late. She had forgotten her sweater, and it was chilly out now that the sun had gone down. She had paced back and forth, waiting for his car to appear, thinking for the millionth time how terrible she felt, having to meet him like this. When were they finally going to come out in the open about their relationship?

"Is something wrong? You seem preoccupied," he said, pulling away from her.

"My mom asked me where I was going tonight," Maria said slowly, fiddling with the belt of her white sun dress. "I told her Lila was having a few people over to see her cousin Christopher. *Then* she wanted to know who I was going with."

"What did you tell her?" Michael asked.

"I told her Winston was picking me up. She knows him because of the campaign, and she thinks he's OK. She wouldn't have believed it if I said I was going out with Jeanie and Sandra again," Maria added.

Michael scowled. "Did you have to tell her you

were going with *him?* You know how much he bugs me."

"Look," Maria said, annoyed. "The truth is, I'm sick and tired of having to tell her anything but the truth! I don't like lying to her, Michael. When are we going to tell our parents the truth about us?"

Michael sighed. "I just don't think my parents are ready for it yet. If we could just wait a little while longer . . ."

Maria sighed and looked out the window on the passenger side. "I thought the whole point of getting engaged was to show our parents how serious we are about each other. How can we let them know that if we keep it a secret?"

Michael's face reddened. "'You're probably just tired of being engaged," he accused her. "Maybe you'd rather we just broke up so you really *could* go out with Winston." Angrily, Michael started up the car.

Maria turned to face him, her eyes filled with tears. "Where are we going?" she whispered. "Can't we stay here and talk about things for a little longer?"

"I promised Lila we'd be over at eight," Michael said tersely. "Let's just go and get this thing over with. I don't see what we have to talk about anyway."

Maria slumped in the passenger seat, the tears brimming over and spilling down her cheeks. She had been wrong to tell Michael about using Winston's name to her mother. She should have known how touchy he was about Winston.

The truth was she had wanted to start a fight. She had been in a bad mood, and she had just been waiting for an occasion to let off steam.

She wasn't sure why, but it seemed that all she and Michael did anymore was argue. It had never been like this before! Sneaking a sidelong glance at him, she noticed his dark, brooding expression as he hunched over the steering wheel. He looked like a complete stranger. So many of the things she had found out about him recently came as a shock to her. Such as his expecting that his wife would never work. Or the way he had talked about disciplining their imaginary child in Mr. Jaworski's class.

A month before, she would have said she knew everything there was to know about Michael Harris. Now she was beginning to think she had been wrong.

They barely even knew each other, yet they had made a commitment to spend the rest of their lives together! She slid farther down on the car seat. She didn't feel like going over to see Lila's cousin anymore. She just felt like going home.

"Hey," Michael said, pulling his car up the long, steep drive to the Fowlers' Spanish-style mansion, set on top of the hill where the most exclusive homes in Sweet Valley were built. The valley lay below them, twinkling with lights, and beyond they could see the ocean. "It doesn't look as if anyone's home. The house is dark. Lila did say tonight, didn't she?"

"Yes," Maria said. "Maybe they've gone out," she added hopefully. "Michael, let's just go home."

Michael gave her an angry look. "That's really typical of you," he said curtly, switching off the engine. "You really take commitments seriously, don't you?"

Maria's eyes stung with tears.

"You do what you like," Michael added. "I'm going to go ring the door bell."

"I'm coming," she muttered, getting out of the car and slamming the door. As she ran to catch up with him, she wiped the tears from her eyes, then took a few deep breaths to compose herself.

Michael was already ringing the door bell. "I think I hear someone," he said a minute later. "Don't you hear footsteps?"

Maria frowned at the darkened house before them. "I don't know, Michael. I don't think—"

But the next instant the door opened, and one of the Fowlers' maids beamed out at them. "Are you Michael and Maria?" she asked. "Come in, come in. Lila's in the drawing room with Christopher. Why don't you follow me?"

Maria had been to several parties at the Fowler mansion before, but she never failed to be impressed by the exquisite beauty of the front hallway, with its grand staircase sweeping up to the second floor. She followed Michael through the cool, dim hallway. The next thing she knew, Lucinda had thrown open a pair of doors, and lights snapped on everywhere. "Surprise!" dozens of voices shrieked.

"Happy engagement!" Lila exclaimed, jumping forward and taking Michael and Maria by the hands.

Michael and Maria stared, first at the room before them and then at each other. The enormous drawing room had been transformed. Silver bells and white balloons festooned the walls. An enormous banner that said "Happy Engagement, Maria and Michael" covered the back wall. A table heaped with desserts stood before them, and in the center was a two-tiered wedding cake, with two miniature figures at the top. The Droids, Sweet Valley High's rock band, were on a platform in the corner, and they struck up

"The Wedding March" when the couple entered the room. Maria and Michael were surrounded by excited classmates, jumping up and down, hugging them, and wishing them the best.

Within seconds Michael and Maria were separated by the crowd. Maria tried to search out Michael's face to see how he was reacting, but he had been dragged off by a group of his friends. And Maria was being led by Lila, who was wearing a magnificent silver dress, to sign her name in the big leather guest book in the corner.

"You're the guest of honor," Lila said happily, clasping her hands.

Maria gave her a sickly smile and wrote her name as neatly as she could in the guestbook.

"This is all such a—such a *surprise*," she managed weakly. Lila looked thrilled.

"We knew you'd love it," she said beaming. "Come on over. Let's get a picture of you and Michael cutting the cake." She called to Bruce Patman to bring Michael to the table.

Maria didn't think she could bear it. It was a nightmare, she decided, an absolute nightmare. How was she going to make it through an entire evening of this?

From the expression on Michael's face as he walked toward her, Maria guessed he was as miserable as she was. But she didn't see any way to escape.

There was a long line of moviegoers waiting outside Valley Cinema for the nine o'clock showing of a new spy thriller. Lydia Pearce, Caroline Pearce's mother, was waiting alone in line while her friend Alice Simon parked the car. She was thinking about several things, among them wondering whether her daughter, Caroline—a junior at Sweet Valley High—was enjoying herself at Lila Fowler's party for Michael Harris and Maria Santelli. To her surprise, she heard a familiar voice behind her. It was Frank Santelli and his wife, Cindy!

"Frank! Cindy!" she exclaimed warmly. "It's been months. I don't think we've seen each other since the benefit dance we all attended at the Sheraton." She kissed Cindy Santelli on the cheek. "I don't know how you do it," she added. "You really do look younger every time I see you."

Mrs. Santelli smiled. "You're just being kind to an old friend," she said, laughing. She checked her watch. "The show should start soon. Did you come with a friend, or are you alone?" Mrs. Pearce had been divorced for years.

"My friend Alice is parking the car," Mrs. Pearce replied. "You know, I haven't even had a chance to congratulate you two about Maria. I hope you don't think I'm awful for not calling, but when Caroline told me, I wasn't certain if you had made a public announcement yet or not."

"Maria?" Mrs. Santelli said blankly, raising her eyebrows. "What do you mean? Congratulate us about what?"

Mrs. Pearce looked confused but said, "Why, on her engagement to Michael Harris, of course. Caroline was thrilled to be in on the surprise party Lila Fowler threw for them tonight," she added. From the expressions on the Santellis' faces she quickly realized she had made a grave error. "Good Lord. You mean you didn't know?" she whispered, horrified. "What have I *done*?" she wailed.

"We certainly *didn't* know," Mrs. Santelli said, shaken. "Frank, do you think this could be true?" She turned back to Mrs. Pearce. "As far as we knew, they weren't even talking! Maria was strictly forbidden to date Michael Harris. If she's been deceiving us . . ."

"Where did you say this surprise party is tonight?" Mr. Santelli demanded. "I think we'd better go over and see what's going on."

"Why, I think it's at the Fowler estate. In fact, I'm sure it is," Mrs. Pearce said, looking upset and nervous. "I can't tell you how sorry I am! If I'd only—"

"Lydia, please excuse us. We're going to run over there right now," Mrs. Santelli declared.

"I want to make a phone call first," Mr. Santelli said darkly. "I want to call Harris. His son is involved in this thing too, and they're going to be as upset as we are."

"That's a good idea," Mrs. Santelli agreed, hurrying after him to some nearby pay phones. "Maybe we can stop over there and talk to them in person on our way."

"I'll tell you one thing," Mr. Santelli said ominously, putting a coin in a pay phone and dialing the Harrises' phone number from memory. "If what Lydia says is true and those kids really did sneak around behind our backs and got engaged, this party tonight isn't going to be the only surprise in store for them!"

Eight

"What a fabulous party!" Lila exclaimed with pleasure, surveying the scene before her.

"If you say so yourself," Jessica muttered. She couldn't forgive Lila for having gone out and buying the silver dress that *she* had found at Lisette's. And to wear it that night! It seemed too cruel.

"Well, you have to admit it's a success," Lila said, nibbling on a tiny white chocolate heart. "Doesn't Maria look wonderful?"

Watching Maria across the room, Jessica nodded. "She looks great in white. I can just see her in her wedding gown," she mused.

Lila sighed with pleasure. "It's just *too* romantic. And to think it's all happening right here, under my very roof."

Jessica rolled her eyes. Before long Lila would

be convinced that she had introduced Maria and Michael to each other!

Just then Dana Larson, the lead singer for The Droids, cleared her throat and picked up the microphone. "And now," she said throatily, "a special song for the couple we're all honoring tonight. This was written just for Michael and Maria. It's called 'Hold on Tight.' "

Everyone cheered. "Dance!" someone cried, and soon everyone was chanting "Dance, dance!" until Michael and Maria came forward, red-faced, and the dance floor cleared for them.

Maria stared up into Michael's face as he moved toward her, but his expression was impossible to read. She took a deep breath as he put his arms around her. Maybe this was all they needed—to hold each other again. Her eyes filled with tears as Dana began to sing.

Hold on to your love, girl.
Hold on tight.
I'm telling you I never knew
What love was, babe, and now there's you.
Hold on to your love, girl.
Hold on tonight.
I'm telling you until I held you close to me
I never knew what joy could be.
And now there's you. . . .
And now there's you. . . .

Maria lay her head on Michael's shoulder, closing her eyes so she couldn't see the crowd of faces watching them. It didn't help. She could tell from the way he was holding her—his arms stiff and awkward, as if he were trying to hold her away—that something in their relationship had snapped, and she wasn't sure it would ever be all right again.

"Are you all right?" she whispered.

"We need to talk," Michael whispered back.

"Let's sneak outside after this," she murmured.

But when the dance ended, the couple was surrounded again. First Lila wanted to arrange a special photo session in front of the cake. Then Jessica insisted on dancing with Michael. Maria watched them move off together.

"Hey," a familiar voice said. Winston had come up behind her, a plate filled with desserts in his hand. "'I don't suppose I could convince you to help me eat some of this stuff, could I?" he said, giving her a shy smile.

Maria smiled despite herself. Winston looked so nice in a navy blue blazer and tan chinos. His hair had been brushed down flat, but one little piece escaped on top. And his face shone from scrubbing. Maria took a heart-shaped cookie and gave Winston a grateful look.

"You having fun?" Winston asked, setting the plate down.

Maria sighed. "Yes," she said at last.

Winston regarded her closely. He took a deep breath and cleared his throat nervously. "Maria," he said, "would you—I mean, do you—will you dance with me?"

Maria burst out laughing. "Sure, Winston," she said. "That would be nice."

He led her out to the crowded dance floor. "I happen," he told her, "to have a penchant for the two-step." The next minute he was leading her in a complicated step that had her out of breath with laughter and exertion in a matter of minutes.

"You're good!" she exclaimed. "How come I never saw you dance like this before?"

"Shyness," Winston said bravely. "The tragic flaw of all real comedians. Actually I was co-erced," he added. "I used to be a terrible dancer. My mother forced me to take a ballroom dancing course—but don't tell anyone."

"I won't. I promise," Maria said laughing. "But you're a great dancer."

"Does that mean we can dance another one?" he asked eagerly.

"Well . . ." Maria looked around uneasily. She didn't see Michael anywhere. "Why not?" she said brightly. The smile on Winston's face made her feel a lot better. In fact, it was fun dancing with him. She couldn't help feeling a little sorry when the next song ended. Winston was doing an imitation of Lila-as-perfect-hostess that made her laugh, and they were waiting for the music to start again when Michael astonished her by taking the microphone from Dana.

"Listen, I don't want to make a formal speech," he said when the crowd had quieted, fixed on the corner where he was standing. "I just want to thank you all for this wonderful party." This met with loud applause, and he raised his hand. He searched the crowd for Maria's face, and her blood ran cold when she saw the expression in his eyes. So he had been watching her dance with Winston! She just hoped he wouldn't say anything to embarrass her. She bit her lip, waiting.

"I also want to thank Maria," he added, staring straight at her. "Sometimes it's hard to tell someone how special she really is—even when she's closer to you than anyone else in the world. The wonderful thing about Maria is that she understands. It's what I love most about her."

The applause this time was profound. Maria's eyes filled with tears. What an idiot she'd been, quarreling with him over silly little things! He still loved her, that was all that mattered. He wasn't jealous of Winston, after all. He loved and trusted her.

"I have one more thing I want to announce," Michael was saying. "This is kind of late in the race, but I've decided to run for the Student Council representative to the PTA. I haven't spoken to Anne Davis, who's in charge yet, but I will first thing Monday morning. And with Maria's help I'm sure I stand a very good chance!"

Maria gasped, her fingers flying to her lips. "What on earth!" she murmured, horrified. How in the world could Michael make an announcement like that? He had never said a word to her about running for Student Council! It didn't even make sense for a senior to run. And she had never said a word about helping him. Her face turned white with anger, then bright red.

"Winston," she said quickly, grabbing his arm, "don't get upset before I explain."

Winston looked at her blankly. "There's nothing to explain," he said dully. "I guess even someone as thick as I am can take a hint." And with that he turned on his heel, crossed the crowded room, and ran out the door.

"Wait!" Maria cried, hurrying after him.

She hadn't gone far when Michael stepped in front of her. "Let him go," he said roughly, grabbing her arm. "Let him go, you hear me?"

Oblivious to the shocked looks on the faces around them, Maria tried to pull free from

94

Michael's grasp. "Let go of me," she said. "You think you own me just because you gave me this ring. Well, you don't! I'm my own person. And you have no right to treat me the way you just did. I made a promise to Winston, and you've made me look like a real jerk!"

"You care so much about what you've promised him," Michael said. "Well, what about what you've promised me?"

"What have I promised you that I haven't done? *You're* the one who won't keep a promise. What about telling our parents? What happened to that?"

Michael's face turned pale as he released her. "If you go chasing after Winston, Maria, it's going to be all over between us. I'm warning you."

Maria stared at him. She was oblivious to the people around them. The room had gone dead quiet, and she was standing perfectly still, staring at him. *Michael, this is Michael*, she thought in a daze. *The guy you love more than anyone in the world. The guy you promised to spend the rest of your life with.*

She stared down at the ring on her hand, her eyes swimming with tears. It seemed to her that all their trouble had begun when they agreed to get engaged. "Michael, I don't think this is right," she whispered, tears brimming over and coursing down her cheeks. "We've stopped having fun together. We fight all the time." She pulled the ring off her finger, struggling to keep her voice calm. "We'll talk later. Now I've got to go apologize to Winston." Fingers trembling, she stretched out her arm and dropped the ring into his open hand.

Michael stared dully after her while she raced out of the room. He barely noticed the rash of concerned questions as his friends patted him awkwardly on the shoulder, leading him over to the couch in the corner, where he sat down.

He stared at the door where Maria had disappeared and then down at the ring in his hand. Finally, his fingers trembling, he put the ring in his pocket and got shakily to his feet. It was at exactly that moment that the Santellis' car was pulling up in the Fowlers' driveway.

Barely half an hour after the Santellis had rung the Harrises' door bell, the two couples were getting out of the Santellis' car in front of the Fowlers' imposing mansion. Everything had happened so quickly that none of them had really had time to think yet, or to realize the magnitude of what had happened. It was the first time any of them had spoken in four years, but it seemed perfectly natural now to be driving in the same car over to Fowler Crest. Alarm over their children had brought the four together, and no mention was made of their quarrel or separation. All that mattered was finding Maria and Michael and learning what had transpired between them.

"Thank goodness Lydia said something to us," Mr. Santelli said earnestly, patting his former business partner on the shoulder as they got out of the car.

"Well, it's a good thing you happend to run into her and that she happened to know what was going on! Otherwise, who knows how far this thing might have gone," Mr. Harris said tersely.

Mrs. Santelli was dabbing at her eyes as they hurried up the walkway to the Fowlers' front entrance. "I don't know how Maria could have behaved so badly, lying to us, sneaking around. . . . She even invented a boyfriend to deceive us! She told us she was seeing some guy named Josh!"

"What about Michael? I think he's much more to blame than Maria is," Mrs. Harris declared.

"I think they're both at fault," Mr. Harris growled, "and I think we all have the right to ask them what in God's name they think they're trying to pull with this crazy talk about getting married! They're only children. How can they even think about marriage?"

Mrs. Santelli threw her arms around Mrs. Harris. "I'm so glad we're in this together," she said tearfully as her husband rang the door bell.

"Santelli, I've got to admit I've missed watching your face when you're going through a crisis," Mr. Harris joked. "It's been a long time since I've seen anyone turn that funny color you get."

"Well, you're not exactly Mr. Cool yourself," Mr. Santelli said, laughing.

"Look, after we've knocked their heads together, why don't we all go out for a drink? I have a feeling we're going to need one."

"As long as we can convince these kids to quit acting so foolish," Mrs. Santelli said.

A maid opened the door and looked at them with surprise. "Good evening," she said. "Can I help you?"

"We're looking for Michael Harris and Maria Santelli," Mr. Santelli said. "We understand there's a party being held here in their honor."

"Yes, come in," the maid said, opening the door. "I'll get Lila."

A minute later Lila flew into the front hall. Her face paled as she saw who was there. "Uh, hello, Mr. and Mrs. Harris, Mr. and Mrs. Santelli," she said nervously. "How nice of you to drop by!"

"Lila," Mrs. Santelli said, "where's Maria?"

"And where's Michael?" Mr. Harris echoed.

Horror-stricken, Lila put her fingers to her lips, and stared at the two couples. "They're —uh, they're—"

"It's all right, Lila," Michael said dully, stepping out into the hallway behind her. "Hi Mom, Dad," he added in a flat, controlled voice.

"Michael, would you mind telling us exactly what is going on here?" Mr. Harris demanded.

"Where's Maria?" Mrs. Santelli cried.

"Why don't you go into the study, where you can talk?" Lila suggested. She led them down the hall to a private, book-lined room and shut the door behind her as she withdrew.

"I'll explain everything to you," Michael said. "But you don't have to worry. Maria's fine, Mrs. Santelli. She's just gone outside with a friend for a few minutes."

"But what's all this nonsense we heard about the two of you being engaged?" Mr. Harris demanded, giving Mr. Santelli a helpless look.

Michael stared at him. "Just that," he said dully. "Just nonsense."

"You mean it isn't true? You're not engaged?" Mrs. Santelli gasped.

"We're not engaged," Michael confirmed sadly. His parents didn't see his left hand tighten around the ring he had withdrawn from his pocket or the tears glinting in his eyes as he sat back in the deep leather armchair in the study, trying hard to think of a way to explain everything in a way that would make some kind of sense.

Nine

To Michael, confronting his parents, seeing them in the same room with the Santellis, and having to make sense out of everything that had taken place between Maria and him seemed like a terrible dream.

He sighed deeply and rubbed his temples. For one brief moment he had considered trying to cover up everything that had happened. But it seemed better to come clean. For one thing, all they had to do was glance in the drawing room, and they would see the big banner congratulating Maria and him on their engagement. No, there was no way to deny that the engagement had taken place. He would just have to do his best to make them realize how terribly sorry they both were for what they had done.

"We made a mistake," he said at last. "A big mistake. It was wrong to lie to you, and it made us both feel terrible. In fact, it was one of the reasons we called things off tonight."

Mrs. Santelli sank back in the chair in the study and closed her eyes for a minute. "So you two really were engaged?" she managed at last.

Michael nodded sheepishly. "We really were. I'm sorry, Mrs. Santelli."

"I wish Maria would come back," Mr. Santelli said sharply. "I'd really like to let her know exactly how we feel about this thing."

"Maria hated lying to you two," Michael said quickly. "I think she hated it even more than I did."

Mr. Santelli shook his head. "Boy, I really feel like a fool," he said slowly. "'You have a daughter, for sixteen years you bring her up in the way you think best, and you find out you barely even know her. She was living under our roof, and we never even guessed any of this was going on!"

"I have to admit I feel pretty much the same way." Mrs. Harris sighed and looked ruefully at her son. "Michael, how could you take such a serious step without consulting us?"

Michael appeared uncomfortable. "Well, you guys were all acting so stupid around each other! Refusing to talk about what happened years ago, making a business mistake into an out-and-out cold war. I guess neither Maria nor I felt like we could turn to you. Not about something like this."

Mr. Harris, red-faced, cleared his throat. "Hmmph," he said, "I guess I haven't been terribly rational about the Santellis, have I?"

Mr. Santelli looked at his wife. "Maybe we didn't exactly encourage Maria's confidence, behaving so childishly ourselves," he conceded.

"Santelli, I'm willing to let bygones be bygones, as the old saying goes," Mr. Harris said stiffly. "That is, if you think you can even tolerate being in the same room with me after what happened four years ago."

Mr. Santelli chuckled. "I'm willing," he said. "As a matter of fact, it's kind of good to see you again, Harris. What have you been doing for the past four years? You look like you've lost a little weight."

Mrs. Santelli dabbed at the corners of her eyes. "I didn't think I'd live to see the two of them talking," she murmured to Mrs. Harris. "I hope you'll forgive me, Sally. I've been as much to blame as my husband in this whole mess!"

The next minute the two women were hugging, and laughter and excited chatter had replaced the tears and recriminations. Michael got to his feet, a sad smile on his face. He had a feeling he could slip away now and no one would notice him.

Ironically, they had forgotten all about Maria and him. They looked like best friends again and would probably end up once more scheming to dance at their children's wedding.

There was only one problem with that, as far as Michael could see: There wasn't going to be any wedding. He had a feeling he and Maria were finished forever.

"Well, we might as well go ahead and have a good time," Jessica said hopefully. "I mean, we're all dressed up, and there's all this wedding cake to eat. We can't just go home, can we?"

Lila looked horrified. "No one can leave!" she shrieked. "This is supposed to be the best party I ever gave." Her brown eyes filled with tears. "You can't possibly *leave*."

"What are we supposed to do?" Jeffrey asked sensibly, his arm around Elizabeth. "I mean, we can't pretend nothing's happened."

"Why not?" Jessica asked gaily, cutting herself a piece of cake. "I'm sure it was just a little spat," she added. "It happens on my favorite soap opera all the time. No engagement counts unless it's been broken at least twice."

"Jess, I don't think this was just a spat," Cara interrupted her. "Michael's in the study now, having some kind of serious talk with the Santellis and his parents. Even if he and Maria do make up, their parents will probably keep them padlocked from now on."

"Still, we can't just stop the party," Lila insisted. "Come on, you guys," she told The Droids. "Play something really upbeat. Let's all start dancing!"

The Droids exchanged glances, and Lila stamped her foot impatiently. "Have fun, everybody!" she shrieked. "I spent a lot of time and money on this party!"

"Leave it to Lila," Elizabeth said, annoyed. "A real display of sensitivity, don't you think?"

Jeffrey stroked her hair tenderly. "Did I ever tell you that you're beautiful when you're angry."

Elizabeth smiled despite herself. "Hey, there's Michael!" she exclaimed as the door to the drawing room opened. The party was in full swing again, and no one seemed to notice him enter.

"I'm going to go talk to him," Elizabeth declared, giving Jeffrey a hasty kiss on the cheek. "Save me a dance, will you?"

"You get *all* my dances," he promised her, giving her a quick hug in return before she slipped away from him and headed for the dark corner where Michael had plopped down on an overstuffed sofa.

"Is this seat taken, or can I join you?" Elizabeth asked gently.

"It sure isn't taken," Michael said bitterly. The next minute his tone changed. "Please sit down, Liz. To tell you the truth, I'd appreciate the company right now."

Elizabeth sat down, not really certain what to say. She and Michael had never been close friends, in part because he was a senior and in part because they had different interests. But she had always liked Michael and really wished she could do something to ease his pain right now. "Are you all right?" she asked gently.

Michael took a long, shuddering breath. "You know, the strange thing is that it's almost a relief. That must sound terrible to you. But the past few weeks . . ." He shook his head. "It's been a lot harder being engaged than I expected it would be." He lapsed into silence again.

"Do you want to talk about it?" Elizabeth asked. "Sometimes an impartial observer is just the right person to pour your heart out to. And I'm a good listener," she added.

Michael smiled at her. "I know you are, Liz. I just don't know if I can be very coherent right now."

"Why don't you try," Elizabeth said softly.

Michael's eyes filled with tears. "It hurts. It hurts a lot," he whispered. "You know, Maria and I have known each other since we were kids. We did everything together. Our parents always teased us because we didn't even go through that boy-girl hating-each-other phase. She was always my best friend—for as long as I can remember."

Elizabeth nodded sympathetically, her blue-green eyes full of compassion.

"And then our parents got into that terrible fight that kept us apart."

"That must have been hard for both of you," Elizabeth whispered.

Michael shook his head. "You know, in a crazy kind of way I think it made it more romantic when Maria and I got together. I mean, our parents had told us we could never talk to or see each other again. But we fell in love anyway, and nothing was going to keep us apart.

"But why did you two decide to get engaged?" Elizabeth wonderd aloud.

"It was always on my mind. I thought—" He broke off, shaking his head again. He was quiet for a moment, then said, "I'm not sure if I really wanted to marry Maria or if it was just because I wanted our parents to know that there was no way they could keep us apart. But once we got engaged, all the romance changed. We started arguing—and, Liz, you have to realize that Maria and I never had an argument before.

Never! Then all of a sudden we were fighting about everything. You name it, and we disagreed about it. You know that project Mr. Jaworski has us working on?"

Elizabeth nodded.

"Well, we couldn't say a word without practically killing each other. You know I never knew how strongly Maria felt about having a career. And she never knew how much I hoped my kids would have a full-time mom around the house. There were lots of things like that. We have different ideas about a lot of things, different ways of doing things. Before, that was part of what attracted us to each other. But once we got engaged the stakes were raised, you know what I mean? If we didn't agree on something we'd panic. We became convinced every argument was sentencing us to doom." He rubbed his forehead. "It was terrible!"

"But do you still love Maria?" Elizabeth asked him.

Michael bit his lip. "I love her—yes. I always will. But I'm not sure I can ever love her in the same way. I think that was part of the reason why I kept getting so angry when she spent more and more time with Winston. I was jealous of him, but I also sensed that Winston was feeling something for her I just couldn't feel anymore. You can see how crazy he is about her. And me—I don't know. After all the fighting, all the worrying—maybe I just want to start all over. Maybe I just want to be her friend and let everything else go."

Elizabeth listened in silence. "I really admire you," she said finally. "I don't think very many guys would be able to admit they'd made a mistake, the way you have. I really admire you for that, Michael." Impulsively she leaned forward and kissed his cheek. "Remember, if you need a shoulder to cry on, or a friend, I'm around. OK?"

"OK," Michael said, swallowing. "And now I think I just want to be by myself for a while. But, thanks, Liz. It really helped me to be able to talk to someone."

Elizabeth patted him on the shoulder as she got to her feet. She couldn't help wondering where Maria and Winston were and what was happening between them.

She just hoped Michael would be able to keep his self-control if they came back inside together.

"Finally!" Jeffrey teased, taking Elizabeth in his arms and swinging her around as The Droids began to play a slow, romantic number.

Elizabeth's eyes twinkled as she looked up at him. "You dance pretty well for a guy who used to live on a tree farm," she said lightly.

"Who taught you how to hold a girl like this, anyway?"

"Haven't you ever heard of instinct?" Jeffrey murmured, pulling her close and kissing the top of her head.

The dance floor was crowded. Next to them Olivia was dancing with Roger, and Lila was dancing with Bruce. Aaron Dallas, the co-captain of the soccer team, gave Jeffrey a nudge as he danced near them with Heather Sanford, his girlfriend. Jeffrey had known Aaron before the Frenches had moved from Oregon to Sweet Valley. He and Aaron had spent a summer together at soccer camp and were good friends. Aaron was in the process of telling Jeffrey an anecdote about a mutual friend from the camp when Roger Collins, who was trying to spin Olivia, accidentally stepped on Aaron's foot. "Hey! Watch it, buddy!" Aaron snapped, his face turning red with anger.

Roger, who was one of the most easygoing boys in Sweet Valley, looked at Aaron in surprise. "I'm sorry, Aaron. I didn't see you," he said pleasantly.

"Well, try to look where you're going," Aaron said coldly, walking off the dance floor and pulling Heather with him.

Elizabeth and Jeffrey looked at each other in

surprise. What was wrong with Aaron? It wasn't like him to make such a big deal out of nothing.

But the next minute The Droids started playing a brand-new rock song, and they forgot everything as they got down to the serious business of having a wonderful time.

Ten

Maria took a deep breath and pushed her curly hair back from her face as she surveyed the grounds before her. It was dark outside, but a silvery glow from the moonlight tipped the trees, and within minutes she could see perfectly. The Fowlers' gardens were magnificent. The air was rich with the smell of blossoms, and a cool night dew soaked her sandal-clad feet as she hurried across the lawn.

"Winston?" she called, but there was no answer.

It was chilly out, and once again she regretted not having worn a sweater. Funny—it felt like ages since she had stood on the sidewalk waiting for Michael to pick her up. She couldn't believe it was the same evening. So much had changed in a few hours.

When Maria ran from the party after Winston, she barely realized the enormity of what had just transpired. Only now, touching her finger where Michael's ring had been, did she begin to realize that it had really happened. They had broken the engagement! She shivered, waiting to feel the terrible sorrow she was sure was about to hit her.

To her surprise, what she felt was closer to relief. It was so beautiful out there, despite the coolness of the air. Suddenly Maria felt an overwhelming sense of joy. It was wonderful to have everything in front of her! Now at last she could see how tense and unlike herself she had been for the past month or so. *Her* interests had ceased to matter. She had been so afraid her parents would find out, and so guilty about lying to them, that she had practically stopped enjoying Michael's company altogether.

And then there was Winston. Maria was astonished by her reaction to Michael's announcement. She knew she had a right to be angry, but her real emotions went beyond anger. Watching Winston's face, she had felt a searing anguish. It pained her to imagine what he must be thinking of her right now. If he thought she had deliberately set him up only to humiliate him . . .

I have to find him, she thought, shivering again.

Could he possibly have run around to the front of the house, gotten his car, and left?

Somehow she didn't think so. By instinct she followed one of the garden paths to a small patio surrounding a fountain. Her heartbeat quickened when she saw a form hunched over on a stone bench. "Winston!" she cried, running forward to meet him.

He looked up incredulously, and she could see he had been crying. "What are you doing here?" he choked out. "I thought you'd be inside, celebrating Michael's announcement about the Student Council."

Maria sat down next to him on the stone bench, still shivering. "Winston, I hope you know me well enough to realize that I had no part in Michael's announcement. I couldn't possibly manage his campaign. After all," she added softly, "I've got my hands full as it is."

Winston stared at her. "You mean—"

"Winston, I would never do a thing like that to you!" Maria cried. "Don't you realize how much I care about you?"

Winston's brow furrowed. He was quiet for a few minutes, mulling something over in his mind. When he spoke again, his voice was much quieter. "Thanks, Maria," he said slowly. "I guess—I guess I was wrong to believe Michael.

I should have stuck around to hear your explanation. But I just assumed . . ."

"I don't blame you for assuming Michael was telling the truth," Maria said earnestly. "After all, you knew we were engaged."

Winston blinked, his eyes fixed on hers. "Did you say 'were'?" he asked.

Maria took a deep breath. She was shivering in earnest now, and Winston noticed for the first time that she was cold. "Take this," he said, slipping out of his navy blue blazer and putting it around her shoulders. She gave him a grateful smile.

"Winston, Michael and I just broke up," she told him. "I hope you're not going to think badly of me for breaking a serious commitment, but it just wasn't right. We're both too young. And ever since we got engaged, all we did was fight. It was horrible. We stopped having fun, stopped caring for each other the way we did before. I guess we made a mistake, that's all."

Winston looked at her very seriously. "You know, I never felt I had a right to say anything about your engagement. I was afraid you'd think I was interfering. But it sounds to me as though you've done the right thing, Maria." He smiled. "I'm glad."

Maria felt very shy all of a sudden. She had stopped shivering now that she had Winston's jacket around her. "Aren't you cold?" she whispered, turning to face him.

Winston was staring at her lips. "N-no," he stammered, red-faced.

Maria reached out and laid her hand very gently against his face. "You look so serious," she whispered. "Winston Egbert, I never knew you could look so serious."

"Maria . . ." Winston choked out.

"Shhh," she murmured, moving her hand to lay her fingers against his lips. "You don't have to say a word."

The next thing she knew he was leaning toward her, and her eyes closed as his lips brushed hers. Her heart hammering wildly, she put her arms around him, touching the back of his neck as his kiss deepened. She couldn't believe this was happening. And yet it seemed perfectly natural. It was the most normal thing in the world, and at the same time, the most wonderful.

"I still can't believe this is happening," Winston declared. It was almost half an hour later, and he and Maria were strolling arm in arm back to the Fowler mansion. "You mean you really liked me all the time? And I was sure you thought I was just one big joker."

"I happen to like your sense of humor," Maria reminded him. "You'd better not turn serious on me, Winston." She giggled. "I've had enough of seriousness for a while, thank you very much!"

Winston laughed. "You can count on my dry wit, my acerbic banter, my humorous sallies. I promise to be a walking comic show, as long as you let me think a serious thought about you every once in a while."

"Every once in a while," Maria agreed. "But that's it!" She shook her head. "I feel like I need to learn to have fun again. You know what I mean?"

"I know," Winston said with mock solemnity. "And I promise to devote myself to fun with the utmost gravity."

Maria burst into laughter. "You're such a nut, Winston," she said playfully.

"I know I'm nuts about you," Winston said, his eyes dancing.

Maria felt happy for the first time in ages. She was relaxed and wanted to have a good time.

But she knew the worst wasn't over. They still had to face Michael when they went inside. And despite Winston's jokes, she guessed he was as nervous about the confrontation as she was.

*　　*　　*

"You know, I've been thinking," Jessica said to her sister as the two shared a delicious strawberry tart. "Does it seem fair to you that Lila should have tons of money while I'm practically destitute?"

Elizabeth rolled her eyes. "Only you could try to discuss redistribution of wealth in terms of who would look better in a silver dress from Lisette's."

"I mean it," Jessica said indignantly. "Honestly, Liz, you never take me seriously. What I've been thinking is that it would be really fun to be rich. *Really* rich. Lila Fowler rich."

"It probably would be—for a while," Elizabeth said absently, taking one last bite of the tart. She wanted to go back and dance with Jeffrey again. Her sister seemed to have latched onto a subject that might occupy her for hours.

"You're not even paying attention to me," Jessica said, pouting. "You're just scanning the room with that haunting where-is-Jeffrey? look on your face."

Elizabeth laughed. "And there he is!" she exclaimed. "I hate to leave you here, wallowing in your poverty, Jess, but I don't think I see a solution to your problem."

Jessica reached for another pastry. "There must be some way."

Just then the door opened, and Maria and

Winston entered the room. A hushed silence fell over the crowd as everyone looked from Winston to Michael and then at Maria.

"Michael," Maria said, taking a step toward him.

Michael tried hard to smile. "You missed an amazing reunion," he told her, with an effort to sound lighthearted. "Our parents found out about the engagement. The four of them came over here to break it up, but they ended with their arms around one another. It looks as though your father and mine might even start up their partnership again."

Maria stared at him for a minute, and the next minute she burst out laughing. Michael, much to everyone's surprise, started laughing too.

"I can't believe it!" Maria gasped. "It just goes to show. Here we moan and groan about their feud, and the minute you and I start a feud of our own, they make up!"

"You should've seen it," Michael told her. "But something tells me you will. I think they're going to be seeing a lot of one another from now on."

Maria's mirth faded as she glanced questioningly at Winston. Michael followed her gaze, and as if he understood what was happening, he got to his feet. "I'm going to be going home now, I think," he said to Lila. "I really feel exhausted. You don't mind, do you?"

Lila shook her head. "Of course not," she assured him, watching Maria and Winston with fascination.

"Winston, can you give Maria a ride home for me?" Michael asked gruffly, putting his hand on Winston's shoulder.

Winston blinked rapidly, a sure sign he was nervous. "Sure," he managed, shifting uncomfortably from one foot to the other.

"Maria . . ." Michael said then, turning to her with a smile.

She stared up at him, wet-eyed. There was so much expression in that smile. It made her heart ache to see that look of love and affection in his face, and to know he forgave her and would still be her friend.

She swallowed hard, her throat aching. It was so hard to say goodbye this way. She knew it must be killing him to leave her there with Winston. But she also knew that this was right for both of them. What she'd had with Michael was too intense, too serious for now. She knew he understood, that he forgave her for everything.

"Friends?" she murmured, taking his hands in hers.

"Best friends," he whispered, squeezing her hands so tightly they hurt.

"Good night, Michael," she said with an effort. She stood on her tiptoes to kiss his cheek. Then she felt as if she had to turn away. It was unbearable to watch him walk through the door.

But at the same time she knew how lucky she was. Michael would always be her friend. She would have a lot of explaining to do to her parents when she got home, but it sounded as if things had worked out incredibly well between them and the Harrises, so perhaps they would be willing to forgive her for having deceived them.

Most of all, she knew she was lucky to have such wonderful friends. And to have Winston, who was looking at her with that shy, lopsided smile that she had come to love. She knew he wanted to take her in his arms but was afraid it might be too soon for that after the wrench of her parting with Michael.

"Listen, Mr. Student Council," she said to him, putting her hand on his arm, "what do you say we see how your dancing is coming along?"

Winston's face broke into a huge smile. And despite the lump in her throat, Maria was happy. It was an evening she would never forget, not as long as she lived. Something precious and rare had ended, but something wonderful was beginning.

She wouldn't deny her grief for Michael, but she wouldn't deny her joy at what was starting between Winston and her. It had been a bittersweet evening, but as Winston took her in his arms, she decided the emphasis was definitely on the *sweet*. And who knew what the future would hold?

Eleven

"All right, group," Mr. Jaworski said, standing in front of the room and surveying his students with a smile. "Today is the follow-up to our family and marriage unit, and as promised, we're going to break up into our pairs again, for the last time. I want you all to discuss what you think you've learned from the project. And again, I'll choose a few couples to come up and present their conclusions to the whole group. Take about twenty minutes to wrap things up, and we'll see what you all come up with."

Laughing and chattering, the group moved back into the "husband and wife" formations that had become familiar to them by now. "I'd say the main thing I learned is that I'd never be satisfied living in the back of a bus with seven children," Jessica said loudly, and everyone laughed.

Lila looked critically at Bill Chase. "I hope he doesn't call on us to present a conclusion," she hissed. "All we've done for the past two weeks is quarrel about why you're still unemployed!"

Bill looked hurt. "I *told* you, Lila—"

"Come on, everyone," Mr. Jaworski interrupted. "Get down to work now. We want to have time to hear your reports."

Maria and Michael looked at each other and smiled. "Well, where do we begin?" Maria asked him.

Michael laughed. "I guess we begin at the beginning. In the first place, I think I learned that there's a lot more to marriage than rings and parties." He shook his head. "You know, I've got to hand it to Mr. Jaworski. To be honest, I never really gave much thought to where we were going to live or what we were going to do for money." He looked rueful. "I think I was acting like a dumb kid in love."

Maria put her hand over his. "Well, Mr. Jaworski's right to make us think about some of the more serious responsibilities that marriage involves. But that doesn't mean he's giving us the whole story. I don't think we were so crazy to act on our instincts. Maybe we were impulsive, but the time was wrong for us. We felt really strongly about each other, though. We can't forget that, Michael."

"I know," Michael said earnestly, looking deep into her eyes. "But I still think we were wrong to talk about marriage. Just because we were in love, that was no reason to rush ahead the way we did. You know, at first I thought our engagement was the way to get our parents to agree to our seeing each other—to force them into it. But then I couldn't get myself to tell them about the engagement, either. I realize now that what I was doing was avoiding any kind of confrontation with my parents. What I should have done ages ago was to go to them and tell them how crazy they were acting and that they couldn't expect us to feel the same way they did. Instead I snuck around behind their backs and acted as dumb as they did! I just continued their cycle of refusing to face reality."

Maria sighed. "We went through some hard times," she mused.

"But some good times, too," Michael reminded her. "You know, if Jaworski asks us to present our conclusions, maybe we *should* say something about romance and love. It seems that his project has left out half of the equation!"

"I think you're right," Maria said. She saw Winston look meaningfully at her across the room and blushed a little.

"He'd sure better treat you well," Michael said gruffly, following her gaze.

Maria lowered her eyes. "He's great," she said softly.

"You know, I never apologized to you for making that dumb announcement at Lila's party," Michael told her. "I never really was going to sign up for the campaign; it wouldn't have made any sense, since I'll be graduating. I just couldn't stand seeing you with Winston. You were dancing together, and it was so obvious what a good time you were having. I acted like a real jerk. Do you forgive me?"

"Of course!" Maria assured him. "A lot of forgiving seems to be going on between the Harrises and the Santellis," she added with a smile. "I hear our fathers are going over to their lawyer's office this afternoon to draw up new contracts. The partnership is back on again!"

"And it's a good thing," Michael declared. "Together they're fantastic. But neither did half as well on his own."

"It'll be fun to have things back to normal again. We'll probably have the old Santelli-Harris softball match this spring," Maria mused.

Michael groaned. "I'm not sure that's really something to look forward to. Remember how many balls I had to throw your bratty little sister before she'd even take a swing?"

"My sister is not bratty!" Maria scolded him with mock severity. The next minute they had both dissolved into laughter. It felt like old times again. They weren't afraid to tease each other about their families.

They were friends again, really friends. And Maria had a feeling that was how it was going to stay.

Michael and Maria were the last of three couples chosen to give their conclusions. They stood in front of the group exchanging nervous smiles as they began their presentation. Maria gave an overview of the tensions that had arisen from her dissatisfaction with her role as a housekeeper. They spent a few minutes discussing the problems that had come up over the crisis involving their imaginary problem son. "I think we learned how important compromise is. And also how difficult it is to agree when two people have opposing ideas about something," she said.

"We also learned how important it is to communicate our differences. In the seminar I finally went along with Michael's decision to use discipline instead of therapy in the case of our problem son. If that had really happened, I would have been really resentful because I was totally opposed to his decision. But I was unable to communicate how strongly opposed I was."

Michael cleared his throat. "Maria and I both agreed that we learned as much from what this project left out as what it put in. Mr. Jaworski, your folders gave us all the information we needed to be a real married couple. We knew our occupations, our family size, our ages, all sorts of things. But your folder didn't say anything about how we felt about each other. You didn't tell us where we met." He smiled fondly at Maria. "Or what made me first fall in love with her. Or what I think about when I can't be with her."

The whole class was very quiet, listening intently to Michael's words. Mr. Jaworski was paying special attention, too.

"We appreciate the project very much because we think most kids our age probably don't give the serious, adult side of marriage all that much thought. But we also want to put in a word for just plain love. The problems we had to deal with were all hard. Without love, they would probably be impossible. Our final conclusion is that a marriage without genuine love and trust just isn't going to make it, however carefully worked out all the other things are."

Michael and Maria took their seats again amid a huge burst of applause, and Mr. Jaworski, after pausing for a moment, began clapping too. "You're absolutely right, Michael," he declared as the bell rang. "I couldn't possibly have said it better myself. Only there are some things you can't learn in a classroom, and some things that just don't make much sense coming from a history teacher."

Michael and Maria exchanged smiles. They had learned their own lesson the hard way. Mr. Jaworski was right. Nothing could have prevented them from making the errors they had made. And they were never going to forget the experience they had been through.

"Winston, don't be nervous. You know your speech backward and forward," Maria assured him. They were hurrying down the crowded hallway to the auditorium, where the four candidates would make their speeches and the election for Student Council representative to the PTA would take place. After the speeches the entire school would vote and decide which would be the best liaison between the school and the Parent-Teacher Association.

Maria could see how nervous Winston was. "I know you're going to be fantastic," she added, giving him an affectionate hug. "Just remember, I'll be right in the front row, waving my Winston This Instant sign."

"I don't know what I'd do without you," Winston replied. "If posters and publicity alone determined the contest, I know I'd win hands down, thanks to the world's greatest campaign manager."

Maria couldn't help sharing Winston's anxiety. The other three candidates, all sophomores, had a real advantage in the race, as they would be able to stay on the council for two years more. Lisa Walton was the one Maria feared most. She was organized and efficient, and she had almost as many posters up as Winston did, with slogans like "Exalt in Walton" or "There's no Fault in Walton." Personally Maria thought the signs were silly, but she knew many of her classmates liked them—and Lisa—a lot. Lisa was a pert, slender girl with straight, blond hair that curled under at the bottom. Neither of the other two candidates seemed much of a threat. Jimmy Reed and Brian Klein, both of whom had entered the campaign late, seemed disorganized, and probably wouldn't be broken-hearted, or surprised, if they weren't elected.

By one-thirty the auditorium was packed. Maria sat in the front row and gave Winston a private victory salute as he came onstage. The expression he returned seemed to say "Wish me luck. I need it." Mr. Roger Collins, the handsome, strawberry-blond English teacher, was in charge of announcing the candidates. As Maria suspected, neither Jimmy nor Brian gave very good speeches. Lisa was next, and she got a huge cheer from the crowd. Her speech was short and to the point and, much as Maria hated to admit it, excellent. Winston was last, and she could tell how nervous he was as he got to his feet.

"Most of you know me as kind of a funny guy," he said. The crowd roared with applause, and Winston put his hand up. "But there's nothing funny about the Student Council. I don't know how many of you are aware of this, because it came as a real shock to me, but do you realize that in the sixties, Sweet Valley High had *no* student council? Students had to stage sit-ins for months before they were allowed to have their own elected representatives."

The auditorium became very quiet. Few people knew this, but everyone seemed interested. "Today most of us take student government for granted," Winston continued. "In many ways that's a good thing. It shows how demanding we are and how high our expectations are. But sometimes we slip a little and become apathetic. My hope is to treat the council as what it originally was seen to be, and what it still can be, with a little work. And that would be a privileged body of representatives actively fighting to represent you on whatever issues you determine are important. With your vote, that's exactly what I'll do."

The applause from Winston's audience was thunderous. "Winston! Winston!" the crowd roared, jumping up and down. Winston this Instant! placards were raised high in the air as people whistled and stamped. From the deafening noise of the crowd, Maria knew Winston had won their hearts. He would undoubtedly win the election in a sweeping landslide.

Later, Maria declared, "I think we need to create a Winston Burger in your honor." She and Winston were in a booth at the Dairi Burger, a popular hamburger place. A gang from Sweet Valley had crowded into the Dairi Burger after the election results were officially announced and Winston was declared the winner. Maria and Winston were in a booth by themselves, but at a table nearby they could see Elizabeth and Jessica Wakefield, Jeffrey French, Lila Fowler, and Bruce Patman.

"I couldn't have done it without you. You know that, don't you?" Winston asked her.

Maria shook her head vehemently. "That isn't true, Winston. I really didn't do very much. This was something you did all for yourself. That speech was really inspired," she added. "It gave me goose bumps!"

"Mr. Jaworski would be proud of me, using history to validate the present. Isn't that what he's always saying?"

Maria lowered her eyes. "Speaking of Mr. Jaworski, I hope you didn't feel uncomfortable in class when Michael and I made that presentation. I had really been hoping he wouldn't call on us."

"I didn't mind!" Winston declared. "In fact, I was proud of you both." He put one hand over hers. "Especially you," he added. "Say, I don't suppose you feel like going to see a movie with me tonight—to celebrate the most action-packed, tumultuous campaign in history?"

"I'd love to," Maria responded eagerly. "You and I deserve a lot of rest and recreation this weekend, Winston Egbert. And the sooner we get started, the happier I'm going to be!"

She was so proud of him she couldn't stop smiling. And she had a feeling that this was just the beginning of something wonderful.

"Jeffrey, you've eaten half my French fries!" Elizabeth exclaimed with mock annoyance.

"Don't you realize sharing food is a sign of great affection?" Ken Matthews asked, leaning over to snatch one of Lila's fries.

Lila gave him a dirty look. "Share your affection with someone else, please, and leave my food alone!"

Everyone giggled.

"I have to admit it, I was surprised by Winston's speech today. Surprised and really pleased," Elizabeth announced. "Wasn't it terrific?"

Everyone agreed, and Jessica was about to chime in when she was interrupted by Aaron Dallas, who had just stormed into the restaurant. He strode over to their table, dragged a chair over, and slumped into it. He was scowling.

"Hey, Aaron," Jeffrey said mildly, "you look like you just lost your best friend."

"Or found your worst enemy," Jessica suggested.

Aaron glared at her. "That's a little closer to the truth." He pulled a folder out of his backpack and threw it onto the table. "Look at that!" he cried angrily.

The folder fell closest to Elizabeth, and she picked it up, staring in surprise at Aaron. She had never seen him so angry before. "What's this? It looks like your English paper."

"That's right," Aaron fumed. "Now open it up and see what that jerk wrote in it, and look at the grade he gave me."

Elizabeth opened the folder to the first page. C- was written in red ink, and a lengthy note followed the grade, explaining the paper's essential problems and suggesting Aaron come in to talk about doing a rewrite. Elizabeth recognized both the handwriting and the careful, sensitive phrasing as Mr. Collins's. She put the folder down. She was surprised by Aaron's anger. It seemed uncharacteristic.

"He's the worst teacher I've ever had," Aaron continued. "He didn't even explain the assignment very well. And then he goes and cheats me on the grade. How am I going to explain this when it shows up on my report card?"

"But he suggests here that you go see him about doing a revision," Elizabeth said. She couldn't help leaping to the teacher's defense. Mr. Collins was one of the most generous teachers she knew, and if he found fault with a paper, she felt there must be a good reason for it. Besides, she hated to see Aaron bad-mouthing Mr. Collins in front of everyone.

Jeffrey picked up the paper and glanced quickly at the comment. "Liz is right, Aaron," he said slowly. "Sounds to me as if you're getting upset for no real reason. Give Collins a break. He isn't trying to hurt you."

Aaron jumped up, furious, snatching his paper out of Jeffrey's hands. "Nobody understands!" he snapped, storming away without as much as a backward glance.

Elizabeth opened her mouth to say something but thought the better of it when she saw the pain in Jeffrey's eyes. Aaron was one of Jeffrey's best friends. He had always been a good friend of Elizabeth's as well. She was willing to give him the benefit of the doubt; he must have a reason to lose control this way.

But she couldn't help wondering what on earth had gotten into him. It wasn't like Aaron to fly off the handle. She had known him for so long, and she'd never seen him lose his temper like this before. She wished there were some way of finding out what was bothering him without making him even angrier.

From the expression on Jeffrey's face, Elizabeth could tell he was feeling the same way. Aaron was obviously in trouble, and they had no idea how to help him.

Can Elizabeth and Jeffrey help Aaron before it's too late? Find out in *OUT OF CONTROL*, Sweet Valley High #35.